THE STUBBORN PORRIDGE

and Other Stories

THE
STUBBORN
PORRIDGE

and Other Stories

by Wang Meng

Introduction by Zhu Hong

George Braziller   New York

First published in 1994 by George Braziller
Copyright © 1994 by Wang Meng
English Translations & Intro. © by Zhu Hong
English Translation © by Yu Fanqin
English Translation © by Cathy Silber
English Translation © by Ai-Li S. Chin
English Translation © by Perry Link
English Translation © by Benjamin Lee
English Translation © by Long Xu
English Translation © by May H. Hong
English Translation © by Jeanne Tai

"The Wind on the Plateau" and "A Winter's Topic" were both
previously published in the *Foreign Languages Press,* Beijing

For information, write to the publisher:

GEORGE BRAZILLER, INC.
60 Madison Avenue
New York, NY 10010

No part of this manuscript may be reproduced
without written permission of the publisher.

Wang, Meng.
     The Stubborn Porridge and Other Stories / Wang Meng ;
translated by Zhu Hong.—1st U.S. ed.
          p. cm.
     A collection of Chinese stories
     ISBN 0-8076-1353-3 : $18.50
     1. Wang, Meng—Translations into English. I. Zhu, Hong.
     II. Title
     PL2919.M39A28   1994   93-47466
     895.1'352—dc20

Contents

Introduction

Wang Meng is the most important writer living in China today. His life and writing career have spanned the period of the Liberation from 1949 to the present. He has suffered and triumphed, and is still actively engaged in life and in writing.

A native of Nanpi county, Wang Meng was born in Beijing in 1934 and joined the revolution at age fourteen. After the communist victory in 1949, Wang worked at the Youth League in the capital city. As a young revolutionary, he was launched on a political career, but he started writing fiction and got himself labeled a "rightist" (enemy category) in his early twenties for "The Young Newcomer at the Organization Department," a short story critical of bureaucracy.

Through the late fifties and early sixties, Wang did various stints of thought-reform-through-manual-labor and finally ended up a political exile in the remote but exotic Uighur-speaking autonomous region of Xinjiang in western China. Thanks to the friendship and protection of the natives among whom he lived, Wang was miraculously unharmed during the Cultural Revolution. He took it upon himself to learn the local language during the mass ritualistic recitations of Mao's *Quotations* and translated Uighur writing into Han Chinese. Wang Meng considers his Xinjiang period one of the most precious experiences of his life and later incorporated it into the series of charmingly humorous stories and sketches known as "The Yili Interlude."

Wang Meng's "rightist" label was removed in 1979 following the death of Mao and the launching of the Deng Era of Reform and Opening-Up. He started writing full-time, becoming one of the most innovative figures in fiction. His better known works—the short stories and novellas such as *Bolshevik Salute*, "Butterfly," "Kite Streamers," "Eye of the Night," and many others—cover every aspect of contemporary life in China. In the early eighties, his name was associated with the introduction of the stream of consciousness narrative technique, sparking a controversy over modernism in Chinese writing.[1] To Wang Meng, stream of consciousness was not a Western gadget but an avenue for explorations of guilt and rethinking for a generation of revolutionaries trying to reorient themselves in the post-Mao era. This is strikingly illustrated in stories in the confessional mode such as "Butterfly," which asks the eternal question "Who am I?" Other major works of this period include the novel *The Movable Parts*,[2] the novella *The Strain of Meeting*,[3] and collections of short stories.

As a result of measures to install merit and expertise in government during the reform, Wang Meng was appointed Minister of Culture in 1986. He said, "Now I am loaded with more and more work, I have less and less time for myself, but I will never put down my pen."[4] And he never did. While serving as Minister of Culture for the 1.2

1. See introduction to *Bolshevik Salute*, trans. with intro. by Wendy Larson (Seattle and London: University of Washington Press, 1989).
2. Included in vol. 2 of *Selected Works of Wang Meng*, (Beijing: Foreign Language Press, 1989).
3. Ibid., included in vol. 1.
4. Wang Meng, "My Love Affair with Writing," in Zeng Zhengnan: *On Wang Meng* (Beijing: Social Sciences Publications, 1987), p. 396.

billion population, he not only kept on writing but entered a new phase in his career.

"It is because life in China has become more complex, its tempo increased," he wrote, "that the themes and rhythms of my stories have changed accordingly."[5] Taking up where he left off with the humor of the Xinjiang interludes, Wang Meng departed from the subjectivity of stream of consciousness and branched off into a wide array of farce, fantasy, fable, allegory, mock heroics, parody, and other experiments in form and language. His tone was now hilarious, facetious, mock-serious, deceptively innocent, ironic, enigmatic. He left the beaten track of the accusatory/expository fiction of the early post-Mao era to create a new kind of writing, where the tone and manner are just as important as the subject matter.

Wang Meng's shorter pieces in the fantastic mode are the first of their kind in contemporary Chinese writing. Some of them hark back to the ancient Chinese fables he parodies, while others (such as "To Alice") belong to the universal family of *Alice in Wonderland* and Edward Albee's somewhat sinister *Little Alice*. He often indulges in reckless, freeflowing wordplay that combines philosophic aphorisms with the earthy folk humor of popular talk shows. With Wang Meng, words sometimes seem to have legs and wander off on their own. Just as Humpty Dumpty could make some words "do a lot more work" than others,[6] Wang Meng's language is self-reflexive, and some words, such as those in "Thrilling" and its sequel, call attention to themselves and generate meaning of their own.

Wang Meng reserves a deep understanding and com-

5. "What Am I Searching For?," in *The Butterfly* (Beijing: Panda Books, 1985), p. 21.
6. Lewis Carroll, *Through the Looking-Glass*, chap. 6.

passion for the sorely buffeted academics of China, who find themselves lost in this new age of galloping materialism. Their frustrations, dilemmas, and weaknesses are brought out superbly in such stories as "The Wind on the Plateau." These mark a significant departure from the sentimental and the pathetic that had dominated stories of victimization during the first phase of post-Mao writing. Wang Meng has eschewed the emotive for the critical spirit of self-inquiry, rationality, transcendence, and abstraction. Therein, too, lies the source of his strength and humor. As he had remarked: "When tears are exhausted, laughter takes over. A sense of humor is a sense of superiority."[7]

The stories in this collection belong to the middle and late eighties, some even to the nineties, when Chinese society evolved into a form of controlled liberalization combined with apparently uncontrollable desocialization. Just as words tend to run away on their own, Wang Meng sees social, economic, and cultural forces also running out of bounds with barely a passing nod to the powers that be. In such short whimsical pieces as "The Twilight Cloud," "Poetic Feeling," and "The Blinking of the Bell," Wang Meng playfully brings out the absurdities and unpredictabilities of the situation. The couple in "Fine Tuning" strive to adjust, but are gripped by "fine tuning" mania under pressure to keep up with the Joneses.

Deeply aware of the contradictions of the age and concerned about his country and its people, Wang Meng still transcends concrete issues in his stories about the living, changing China. Rather, he relies on metaphor to reflect on the complexities and relativity of human affairs. Whether

7. *The Chinese Western*, trans. with intro. by Zhu Hong, (New York: Ballantine, 1988, 1991), p. 140.

4

it is the quest for the ideal family menu ("The Stubborn Porridge"), or the last word on the great "bathology" debate ("A Winter's Topic"), he rejects clear-cut, black-and-white stereotypes and suspends judgment. Reform, elections, meritocracy, tradition, family, academic politics, generation gaps, fashionable theories, Chinese medicine, Western technology—Wang Meng calls everything into question, exposes it to scrutiny, and turns it into entertainment in what may be called (for lack of a better term) "dialectic absurdism." "Heat Waves of Summer" makes a subtle analogy between the sometimes misplaced fervor of reform measures and an aborted liaison, both brought on by a passing "heat wave." He sees many things as "heat waves" that come and go—"Is it subtle thinking or complicated nonsense?" to borrow from the title of his October 1993 talk at Harvard. Wang Meng relies on the down-to-earth common sense of people like those in "The Stubborn Porridge" who finally stop racking their brains over "the great eating debate" and manage to feed their bellies in spite of "theories and terms and methodology." Without resorting to diagnoses or prescriptions, Wang Meng evidently is confident that "all things in heaven and earth find their own balance" ("The Stubborn Porridge").

Milan Kundera, in writing about life under communism, conveyed in a single untranslatable word—"litost"— that peculiar "state of torment caused by a sudden insight into one's own miserable self."[8] Wang Meng's "dialectic absurdism" is a unique synthesis of the hope, elation, resilience, defiance, frustration, scepticism, anxiety, and bewilderment of a people desperate to leave the past behind them, though not sure exactly where they are heading. It marks a

8. Milan Kundera, *The Book of Laughter and Forgetting*, (New York: Alfred A. Knopf, 1980) p. 122.

new phase in contemporary Chinese writing and is a significant contribution to the international writing associated with Kundera and Bulgakov.

Wang Meng stepped down from office after 4 June, 1989. In a country known for stringent censorship, which had taken away twenty years of his life for an innocent short story, and at a time when the suppression of dissent was fresh in people's minds, he decided to sue the official publication of the Writer's Union for its libelous attack on "The Stubborn Porridge," (also known as "Hard Porridge") Therein lies the reason why "much of Beijing's intellectual and cultural world is transfixed by the remarkable spectacle of a victim fighting back, particularly because he is one of China's most celebrated writers and a former Minister of Culture."[9] Wang Meng is not beyond a shot of the mischievous, too, writing a sequel to his work under attack, notably, "Capriccio à Xiang Ming" in response to an attack on "Thrilling" by a scribbler who had totally misread the piece.

Readers nationwide gave their own verdict of the "porridge controversy" in increased circulation of the story and "porridge mania" across the country, with articles dealing with porridge from every conceivable angle: "Porridge Fun," "Porridge Cure," "Textual Porridge," "Porridge Flavor North and South," "Porridge, the Sustenance of the People." It was even suggested that 1991 be named the "Year of Porridge."

Wang Meng has been honored with many literary prizes at home and abroad, and his works have been translated into all the primary Asian and European languages. But he thinks that the best thing that has happened to him is that he has kept on writing.

Wang Meng has gone through the "state of torment"

9. *New York Times* 20 November 1991, A4.

and left it behind him. He has done more than "survive communism and even laughed."[10] He is still right there: surviving, laughing, and telling the world.

—Zhu Hong

10. Slavenka Drakulic, *How We Survived Communism and Even Laughed*, (New York: W. W. Norton, 1991).

The Stubborn Porridge

The official members of our family are: Grandfather, Grandmother, Father, Mother, Uncle, Aunt, I, my Wife, my First Cousin on my Father's side, my First Cousin's Husband, and my lovely, lanky Son. Our ages are respectively eighty-eight, eighty-four, sixty-three, sixty-four, sixty-one, fifty-seven, forty, forty . . . and sixteen. An ideal of structural gradation.[1] And then we have an unofficial member, unofficial but indispensable—our housekeeper, Elder Sister Xu, age fifty-nine. She has been with us for forty years, and we all call her Elder Sister Xu. A clear case of all men born equal with natural rights.

We lived together, peaceably and united as one.[2] On all issues big and small, such as whether this summer is hotter than usual, whether to drink Dragon's Well tea at eight yuan an ounce or green tea at forty fen an ounce, or which brand of soap to use—the gentle Violet or the intimidating Golden Armor—Grandfather had the last word. Strifes and contentions, overflowing rhetoric, and closed-doors conspiracies were absolutely unheard of. We even shared the same hairstyle, distinguishing between male and female, of course.

1. An allusion to the practice of arranging takeover of key posts on a diminishing range of age.
2. A reference to the official slogan "Stability and Unity" as the ultimate good.

For the last several decades, we all got up at ten past six in the morning. At 6:35 A.M., Elder Sister Xu would have our breakfast ready: toasted slices of steamed bread, thin rice porridge, pickled turnip heads. At 7:10 A.M. we would all set out, respectively, to work or to school. Grandfather had already retired, but still showed up every morning at the Neighborhood Committee as officer on duty. We all came back at 12:00. By then Elder Sister Xu would have lunch waiting for us, bean curd–paste noodles. After a short nap, we would all get up at 1:30 P.M. and start off again, respectively, to work or to school. Grandfather, however, slept until 3:30 P.M. Then he would get up, wash his face and brush his teeth for the second time, and sit on the sofa to read the newspapers. At around 5:00 P.M., Grandfather and Grandmother and Elder Sister Xu would have a consultation about the menu for supper. This was a daily routine which never lost its interest for the three participants, although the results hardly varied from one day to the next. Let's say rice for supper tonight. As to dishes, let's make it one meat, one half-meat half-vegetable, and two vegetables. As to soup, let's skip it today. Or let's say have soup today. After this discussion, Elder Sister Xu would go into the kitchen and get down to work, chopping away. Thirty minutes later she was bound to pop out: "To think that I could have forgotten! I had not asked about the pork in the half-meat half-vegetable. Should it be sliced or shredded?" Well, there is no denying the importance of the issue. Grandfather and Grandmother would look at each other significantly and one of them would say: "Might as well be sliced." Or they might say: "Let's make it shredded." And their decision would be faithfully implemented.

Everybody was satisfied with this life, Grandfather first and foremost. Grandfather had suffered in his youth and would often admonish us: "A full stomach, unpatched clothes, good health, a well-furnished home, and all the generations living together—why, this is even beyond the dreams of landlords in the old days. Now you people, don't let it go to your heads. What do you know of the pangs of hunger?'' But Father and Mother and Uncle and Aunt would protest that they knew full well the pangs of hunger.[3] When you are hungry, they said, your chest and stomach go into constrictions, your head dangles, your legs wobble. They added that extreme hunger felt the same as overeating, you want to throw up. Our whole family, headed by Grandfather and Grandmother, were followers of the maxim that Happiness lies in Contentedness, and were faithful upholders of the existing system of things.

But lately, things have been changing. We were constantly assailed by new fads and fashions. Just within the last few years, a color TV, a refrigerator, and a washing machine made their way into our home. Besides, my Son's speech was often interspersed with English. Grandfather was most liberal and open-minded, garnering a stock of new terms from the papers after his daily nap, or from radio and TV programs after supper. He would often take a poll of public opinion. ''Now is there anything to be reformed or improved in our family life?'' he would ask.

Everybody would hasten to say no, especially Elder Sister Xu. She prayed that this kind of life would go unchanged from day to day, year to year, generation to generation without end. My Son came up with a proposal. He blinked his eyes real hard as if there was a worm inside. He proposed that we buy a cassette recorder. Grandfather agreed, acting on the principle that heeding advice led to the attainment of perfection. So there was an addition to our

3. An allusion to the famine following the Great Leap Forward of 1958, brainstorm of the late Chairman Mao Zedong.

family belongings in the shape of a Red Lamp–brand cassette recorder. At the beginning we were all thrilled. One would say a few words, another sing snatches of Peking opera, this one would imitate a cat's meowing, while another would read a passage from the papers, and we would tape it and play it back. How we enjoyed it all! And to think that Grandfather's father and grandfather had never known the existence of such a thing as a cassette recorder. But after the first few days, the thing began to pall. The songs on cassette which we played on the machine did not sound as nice as those on radio or TV. The cassette recorder was put aside to collect dust. Everybody realized that these new gadgets had their limitations after all. They were not as durable as the old "song box." Nothing could take the place of tradition, nothing could compare with order and harmony within the family.

That same year, the uneventful pace of our family life was ruffled by an order cancelling the long noon break for napping, to be replaced by a short forty- to sixty-minute break. The compensation was that each work-unit would provide free lunch. A mixed blessing for us, however. We were glad about the free lunch. But on the other hand, we were distressed by the change, and could not adjust. After two days of free lunch, we were all affected with constipation and other symptoms of the Heat Syndrome. Then it was announced that free lunch would be cancelled, and we were left wondering, what's going on anyway? What were we to do? Grandfather admonished us always to take the lead in keeping on the path shown to us by the government. So there was a big fuss over buying lunch boxes, preparing lunches, and taking them along to the office. Elder Sister Xu suffered from insomnia, toothache, eye infection, and accelerated heartbeat. It wasn't long before some work units prolonged the noon break. Others did not officially revert to the long noon break but surreptitiously delayed the start of the afternoon work hour, though sticking to the early hour for leaving work. Our family reverted to our lunch of bean-curd paste noodles. Elder Sister Xu was immediately cured of all her complaints, no more eye infections, no more toothache, her sleep was on schedule, and her heartbreak under perfect control at 70 to 80 beats a minute.

But the surging waves of reform rolled onward and the rousing winds of change swept all before it. All creatures under heaven were in motion, all affairs on earth in transition. Just as our fellow creatures right and left, uplifted by self-examination and restrained in sorrow, were putting the past behind them and mapping out new dreams of reform and regeneration, friends and relatives who used to praise us as a model family and an exemplary household now started urging us to move with the times. It seemed that new models of family life had cropped up in Guangdong, or Hong Kong it may be, or even the United States.

Grandfather took the lead in proposing that we change from a Monarchy to a Cabinet system. The members of the Cabinet would be nominated by Grandfather himself, to be approved by the Plenary Session of the Family Congress, including Elder Sister Xu, a nonvoting member. The reins of government would be rotated among the official members of the Cabinet. Except for Elder Sister Xu, Grandfather's proposition was unaminously approved. Father was designated to take over the reins of government and entrusted with the Reform and Modernization of our Menu.[4]

The fact was, Father had always had his food ready for him and his work cut out for him. Which meant that he ate what was put in front of him and did whatever part of the household duties assigned to him. Now saddled with the

4. Borrowed the term from the Meiji Reform of Japan.

momentous task of overseeing the Menu for the whole family, he was embarrassed and overwhelmed. When challenged by such major issues as what kind of tea leaves to buy, or to choose between sliced or shredded pork, he would invariably turn to Grandfather. He would never say anything without quoting Grandfather: "The Patriarch said to buy Chrysanthemum-brand mosquito incense." "The Patriarch said not to make soup tonight." "The Patriarch said not to use detergent for dishwashing. Might be poisonous, these chemicals. Hot water and baking soda, much cleaner, and cheaper too."

Trouble followed immediately. Elder Sister Xu would ask Father whenever she had a question, and Father would ask Grandfather, coming back to Elder Sister Xu with the Patriarch said so and so. So far as Elder Sister Xu was concerned, she might as well go directly to Grandfather. But that might hurt Father's feelings and she was also afraid to bother Grandfather. Grandfather did not want to be bothered with trifles, and had repeatedly ordered Father: "Make your own decisions! Don't always come to me!" So Father would go back to Elder Sister Xu with: "The Patriarch has said that I am to decide. The Patriarch has said that he doesn't want to be bothered."

Soon there were murmurs from Uncle and Aunt. Murmurs against what? Nobody knew for sure. Probably impatience with Father's ineptness. Perhaps a suspicion that Father was using Grandfather's name in vain, "fabricating the edict of the Emperor," as the saying goes. Possibly also disaffection with Grandfather for not completely giving up the reins of government, or annoyance at Elder Sister Xu's nagging. And finally, resentment at everybody else for okaying the Cabinet system and confirming someone like Father as a member of the Cabinet.

Grandfather became aware of the murmurs, and formally invested Father with authority, admonishing him at the same time that the delegation of power to lower levels was in keeping with the times. Father, cornered, promised not to invoke Grandfather's name in future dealings. But having gotten his Mandate, he went ahead and delegated power to Elder Sister Xu to decide between soup or no soup, and shredded or sliced pork.

Elder Sister Xu would not be empowered. How can I decide, she snivelled between tears. She was so overwhelmed by the burden of responsibility that she missed a meal. The family encouraged her: "You have worked so long in our family. Power should go with office. You just take over, we are all behind you. Go ahead, buy whatever you like, cook whatever you like, and we'll eat whatever you put before us. We have faith in you."

Elder Sister Xu smiled through her tears and thanked everybody for showering her with such honors. So for a while, things went on as before. But soon murmurings began to be audible, as it was plain that Elder Sister Xu did not have the true Mandate. Imperceptible signs of disrespect gradually evolved into outright complaints. It began with my Son, was taken up by my First Cousin and her Husband, and soon even I and my Wife were infected. At first, it was just satiric comments: "Our menu has been lying there unchanged for four decades. Must have antique value by now." "Such single-minded adherence to convention! Such rigidity! Rejection of all change!" "Our family's life-style is a fine example of living in a time capsule!" "Elder Sister Xu's perspectives are so restricted! Lack of culture, of course. She's all right as a person, but hopelessly backward. To think that now, in the eighties, our living standards must adapt to *her* level!"

Elder Sister Xu had no inkling of what was simmering around her. On the contrary, she began to enjoy her new status and went ahead with her own version of Reform. In

14

the first place, the two platefuls of pickled turnip heads for breakfast were reduced in quantity to one, only served up in two plates. The sprinkling of sesame oil over the pickles was abolished. The bean-curd paste for lunch which used to be stir-fried with a bowl of pork cubes was now changed to plain bean-curd paste cooked in water. The soup which used to be served on alternate days now turned up only once a week. And when it did appear, it had changed from egg drop soup to plain water with a dash of soy sauce, sprinkled with chopped spring onions. With the money thus saved, she went and bought royal jelly as a gift offering to Grandfather. So! She was squeezing us to curry favor with Grandfather! And we could only stand by helplessly and fume! More in-furiating, according to my Son's report, was the fact that after making the plain soup, she would scoop out a bowl with the thickest sprinkling of chopped spring onions for herself, before the family was served. On another occasion, she was seen cracking melon seeds as she chopped the vegetables. She must have embezzled the family's public funds! ''Power corrupts. Absolute power corrupts absolutely!'' My Son had found his newly acquired theory fully validated.

From Father downward, nobody intervened to put a stop to the murmurs. Taking silence as acquiescence, my Son fired the first shot, choosing the moment when Elder Sister Xu was enjoying her clandestine soup. ''Enough is enough! I'm sick of your substandard meals. And saving the pick of the chopped spring onions for yourself! That's the limit! Starting tomorrow, I want everybody to enjoy a modern life.''

Elder Sister Xu cried and made a scene, but nobody did anything to stop the rush of events. We felt that my Son should have a chance. He was young, fired with ideas, and full of energy. It seemed the time was ripe for the likes of him to take over. Talent must be fostered, after all. Of course I and members of the family tried to console Elder Sister Xu. "You have cooked in our family for the last forty years, your achievements outweigh everything else. Nobody can take that away!"

My Son broke into an orgy of rhetoric: "Our family's way of eating has persisted unchanged for forty years. The problem does not stop here. What is worse, there is too much carbohydrates and too little protein. Lack of protein affects our growth, reduces the generation of antibodies in the white blood cells. The result is the weakening of the constitution of the population as a whole. People in the West take in seven times more protein than we do. In terms of animal fat their intake is fourteen times more than ours. We are not as tall, nor as strong, nor as energetic as they are, not to mention body shape. They sleep once a day, six hours at the most, yet see how they carry on nonstop from morning to night. Look at us. Even with our daily nap, we are still lumps of inertia. You might say, how can we compare with developed countries? All right then, let's take our own national minorities. Now let me tell you something: the food structure of us Hans cannot compare with that of the minorities—you can't say that they are economically more developed that we are, can you? Our intake of protein is far lower than that of the Mongols, the Uighurs, the Hassacks, the Koreans of the north, or the Tibetans of the southwest. Now how can you expect to survive without a change in our food structure? Take breakfast for instance—the everlasting slices of steamed bread and thin porridge with pickles to go! Heavens! Is this the kind of breakfast fit for middle-income urban residents of China in the eighties of the twentieth century? How shockingly primitive! Porridge and pickles—perfect symbols of the Sickman of Asia. This is an insiduous form of genocide! A disgrace to our ancestors! This is the root of the decline of Chinese civilization! Emblematic of the backward culture of the Yellow

16

River! If we had eaten bread and butter instead of porridge and pickles, would we have lost the Opium War to the British in 1840? Would it have been necessary for the Empress Dowager to flee to Chengde during the invasion of the Eight Allied Armies in 1900? Would the Japanese Army have dared to incite the September 18 Incident in 1931? Would not their regiments have collapsed in fright if they had seen our lips smeared with butter and our chins dripping with cream? If in 1949 our leadership had outlawed all porridge and pickles and ordered the nation to shift to bread and butter and ham and sausage and eggs and yogurt and cheese and honey and jam and chocolate thrown in, wouldn't we have achieved a leading place in the world community long, long ago in terms of national growth rate, science and technology, art, sports, housing, education, and number of cars per capita? Getting down to basics, porridge with pickles is the root of our national disasters, the fundamental reason for the ultrastability of our unchanging feudal system! Down with porridge and pickles! So long as porridge and pickles are not wiped out, there is no hope for China!"

The speaker was fired and the audience moved. I was seized with threefold sentiments of surprise, joy, and fear. Surprise and joy that without my realizing it, my Son had actually outgrown his slit pants and no longer asked me to wipe his bottom for him. He had enriched his mind so massively, accumulated so much new learning, raised such searching questions, and seized on such a crucial issue! I deeply felt that heaven and earth should give way to my Son. It could be truly said of him that, nourished on porridge and pickles, he harbored visions of butter and ham. It is no exaggeration to say that he had poured forth the sweeping winds of modernization, enveloping everything within the four dimensions. Truly may it be said, the young are to be feared, the world is theirs.

But I was also alarmed. I feared the way he had seized on all current abuses with his wit and annihilated everything with a sentence. I feared that this kind of exaggerated rhetoric was just so much air and would end in nothing. According to my half century of experience, whenever a complex problem was neatly dissected and laid out in black and white, whenever the solution to overwhelming odds was easy and ready-made, I am afraid that as soon as the first ecstasy of analysis and prescription was over, the agent would be reduced to impotence. With this one and only twig to carry on the family tree, Heaven forbid that he should be so afflicted!

Just as I had anticipated, my First Cousin snorted and mumbled under her breath: "All very nice indeed! If we had had that much bread and butter, we would have achieved modernization long ago!" "What!" my Son, still on the crest of his zeal, shot back at his aunt. "Khrushchev had proposed his 'stewed beef and potatoes' brand of socialism in the sixties, and now you are proposing a 'bread and butter' version of modernization! What a coincidence! Modernization, let me tell you, is the automization of industry, the collectivization of agriculture, the ultramodernization of science, the conversion of defense to multiple civil uses, the whimsicality of thought, the impenetrability of terms, the distortion of art, the limitless multiplication of controversy, the paring down of academe, the mystification of concepts, and the transformation of man into a set of paranormal functions. The sea of 'Ization' is boundlessly shifting, butter gives it shape. The garden of delights is inaccessible, but bread builds a bridge. Of course bread and butter will not be showered down from the skies like bombs from an imaginary enemy, don't you think I know that much? What do you take me for, an idiot? But we must raise the question, we must set up a goal. A nation without a goal is like a man without a head, never knowing its own potential . . .''

"Well said, well said,'' Grandfather interjected. ''The two of you are moving in the same direction. No need to argue.'' And so the controversy died down.

My Son believed in action. Right away the next morning, bread and butter, eggs, milk, and coffee were on the table. Grandfather and Elder Sister Xu simply could not take coffee and milk. Uncle thought of a solution: chopped spring onions fried in a wok, add peppercorn, cassia bark, fennel, ginger skin, pepper, seaweed, and dried hot pepper; when the mixture is cooked, add a dash of Cantonese soy sauce, then pour into coffee and milk. It's bound to drown out the barbarian stink. I tried a mouthful, it worked; the taste of coffee and milk was not discernible anymore. I also wanted to add this potion to my own cup of coffee, but seeing my Son's glare, I sacrificed my palate for his sake and gulped down the stinking mess. Alas, these little Emperors of the Four-Two-One Syndrome—four grandparents and two parents revolving around the single child—what are they leading our country into?

In three days, the whole family was in an uproar. Elder Sister Xu was in the hospital with acute diarrhea. The doctors suspected colon cancer. Grandmother was afflicted with nervous hardening of the liver. Grandfather was hopelessly constipated. Father and Uncle, filial sons that they were, tried to ease his bowel movement by breaking up the constipated mass with bamboo chopsticks stuck up his rectum, but to little effect. Our First Cousin had to be operated on, while her Husband's gums were all infected and swollen. My wife would throw up after every meal, and having got rid of her Western breakfast, would sneak away to her parents' home for thin porridge and pickles—keeping it a secret

19

from our Son, of course. A greater cause for alarm was the fact that my Son had run through our monthly budget in three days. He announced that without extra funds, he would not even be able to provide thin porridge for the rest of the month. Affairs having come to this, I had no choice but to stick my head out and join with Father and Uncle to depose my Son and restore the family life to normal.

Father and Uncle had no option other than to look to Grandfather, and Grandfather had no option other than to look to Elder Sister Xu. But Elder Sister Xu was in the hospital, and announced that even after she was released from the hospital, she would not cook. If anybody thought her a burden, she declared, they could send her packing. Grandfather deluged her with a thousand protestations, reasserting his own philosophy of putting personal loyalty and obligation above all else. He assured Elder Sister Xu that she was preeminent on both counts, closer than Grandfather's own kin, valued above his own flesh and blood, deserving both loyalty and obligation from the family. Grandfather vowed that Elder Sister Xu was part and parcel of the family to her last breath. That if we were down to our last steamed bread, Elder Sister Xu would have a bite. That if we were down to our last glass of water, Elder Sister Xu would have three sips. That if we made a fortune, Elder Sister Xu would have her share. That if our luck went down, Elder Sister Xu would still be taken care of. That such a thing as using people first and then kicking them out was beyond contempt. Grandfather threw himself into protestations, words rolling, tears streaming. Elder Sister Xu took in every word, heart and liver warming, eyes overflowing, nose dripping. Things came to such a state that the medical staff on duty decided that this communication was detrimental to the patient's condition and Grandfather, still teary, had to leave.

Back home, Grandfather called a Plenary Session of

the Family Congress. At the meeting, he announced that though he was getting on in years, he did not hold rigid ideas about what to eat and like matters, even less would he harbor vaulting ambitions toward autocratic rule. "But," he pointed out, "since you insisted that I do something about the situation, I had no choice but to look to Elder Sister Xu. I found her heartbroken by your complaints, and her stomach wrecked by my Great-Grandson's Western breakfast. So I give up. Eat what you like. As for me," he added, "it is just as well that I starve to death."

At this, we looked at each other and all rushed in to assure Grandfather that he had done a good job: for a good fifty years now, old and young each had had their place, four generations coexisting under one roof. My First Cousin declared that she would cook for Grandfather, that is to say, she herself, her Husband, Grandfather, Grandmother, and Elder Sister Xu would be one Eating Unit. Father hastened to declare that he would make up a second Unit with Mother, but that he would have to exclude me and my Wife, on account of our New Wave Son who would not fit in with their eating habits. I also declared that I was with my Wife, while Uncle and Aunt banded together. My Son was a single-member Unit. First Cousin's Husband seemed pleased and remarked: "Might as well eat separately, more like a modern life-style; four generations eating together is so old-fashioned, like something out of *Dream of the Red Chamber*. And anyway, so many people eating together around one table makes such a crush, not to mention the danger of catching hepatitis." My First Cousin retorted: "But where can you find such a big family in the U.S.? Can you imagine them overcoming the generation gap and sitting together to a meal?" An expression of resignation seemed to flicker across Grandfather's face.

Barely two days had passed before the arrangement

to eat in separate Units was in disarray. At around 11:00, my First Cousin's Unit would take over the kitchen. Armed as she was with the authority and prestige of Grandfather, we could only stand by and look on longingly. After Grandfather came Father's turn, and after Father came Uncle. When my turn came round, it was already 2:00 in the afternoon. I had to rush to work without lunch. At supper, the cycle was repeated. Something had to be done. We talked about the possibility of each Unit setting up its own stove. More gas tanks were out of the question. To acquire the one we now have for the whole family, we had made fourteen personal visits, hosted seven dinners, and bestowed two painted scrolls, five cartons of cigarettes, and eight bottles of wine as gift offerings, and the whole process had taken thirteen months and thirteen days. You could say that we had put as much energy in it as firstborn infants in sucking, or old men in shitting. Buying stoves was also an arduous process. Besides, even if you do get a stove, you need a certificate to buy coal brickettes. No certificate, no brickettes. And even if you do get hold of the certificate and buy the brickettes, there was nowhere to store them. If we decide to set up four separate stoves according to the Modern Consciousness, we need to expand the kitchen by thirty square meters. Or better, to install four extra kitchens. Or even better, to set up five individual apartments. Man's appetite for consumption is like a galloping fire. The current alarm at overconsumption in the press is just a waste of breath. The more you talk, the hotter it gets. Suddenly it occurred to me like an epiphany that all this twaddle about Modern Consciousness and Renovating your Concepts and the Right to Privacy was just so much hot air if you do not build more houses.

Discussion on the Soft Science of separate stoves got us nowhere. Meanwhile, a whole tank of coal gas was exhausted in nine days. Starting this year, the Petroleum and

Gas Company had introduced the new method of issuing certificates for gas supply. We were limited to a dozen or so tickets per year, so every tank had to last at least twenty-five days to ensure cooking and hot water for the entire family all year round. If we ran through one tank in nine days, our whole quota of certificates would not last more than four months, and what were we to do for the other eight months of the year? This was not only destroying the order of our own lives, but subverting national planning!

We were completely dismayed: sighs, complaints, gossip, and rumor filled the air. Some said we could live on uncooked mixed dough. Some said each Unit's cooking should be limited to seventeen minutes. Some said this separation into eating Units was a clear case of the relations of production outrunning the level of development of the forces of production. Some said the more you reform the worse it gets, that we were much better off when Grandfather's word was law and Elder Sister Xu ran the show. Others cursed the U.S., saying the Americans were like a pack of wild animals with no family and not a shred of filial piety. We have our own excellent tradition of familial virtues, why should we learn from the Americans? Why indeed? But what were we to do? After the last episode, we were ashamed to bother Grandfather again with questions and requests, so we went to my First Cousin's Husband.

First Cousin's Husband was the only member of the family who had had a taste of things foreign. During the last few years, he had ordered two suits, bought three ties, and been in the U.S. for six months of "further studies," in Japan for a ten-day visit, and in the Federal Republic of Germany for a tour of seven cities. Well informed, carrying himself with an air, capable of saying "Thank you" and "Excuse me" in nine different languages, he was considered the true scholar in the family. But coming from outside the clan, he was aware of his inferior status and always behaved with discretion and modesty, thus winning our deep respect.

On this occasion we were at our wit's end, hopelessly mired in the strange circle of dilemmas. Seeing the urgency of the case and the sincerity of our supplication, he returned trust for trust and delivered the goods.

"As I see it," my First Cousin's Husband began, "the basic issue is the system. Whether we eat sliced steamed bread or not is of no account. The basic issue is not what we eat, but who makes the decision and by what process this decision is arrived at. Through the feudal patriarchal order? By seniority of age and rank? By leaving things to anarchism? By relying on whims and caprices of the moment? According to published menus? Is accepting the inevitable a form of predestination? Let me tell you, the Key is Democracy. Without Democracy, you won't know the taste of what you're eating no matter how good it is. Without Democracy, nobody will make a stand for reform no matter how vile the food is. Without Democracy, one can eat only in an unenlightened way, not knowing the sweetness of sugar nor the bitterness of bittermelon. How can one tell the difference, when neither the sweetness nor the bitterness has anything to do with one's own choice? Without Democracy, one would be passive and dumb. The Subject would lose consciousness of the act of eating, and the Eating Subject would be alienated from its nature and reduced to a manure manufactory. On the other hand, the Eating Subject may be lost in confusion, now capricious, now indiscreet, grasping at palpable gains and seeking only short-term effects, exuding hostility to its neighbors, and ultimately turning into a stomach-flaunting, headless monster. In a word, without Democracy there is no choice, and without choice the Conscious Subject is alienated from its own identity."

We listened in awe, nodding in agreement. It was as if

an enlightening fluid had been injected into our brains.

Uplifted by our reception, my First Cousin's Husband continued: "The seniority system is all right for a stagnant agricultural society. One might even go so far as to say that it brings order, the sort of order suited to illiterates and idiots. I suppose people born with lower IQs will accept this kind of order—dull, sluggish, moribund. But it kills competition, it stifles man's initiative, creativity, and changeability. We all know that without change there would have been no mankind, we would still be apes. Moreover, the system of seniority represses the young. A man's energy is at its most vital, his mind at its most active, his aspirations at their most ardent before the age of forty. Yet in reality, at this age they are all languishing at the bottom . . ."

My Son interpolated: "How true!" A few tears trickled down his cheeks.

I signaled him to stay out of this. The fact is, ever since the fiasco of his Western breakfast program, his image had been somewhat damaged. People tended to associate him with risky adventures, empty theories, and even a hint of the Red Guard rebel spirit—more hindrance than help in any undertaking. The other members of the family, including my First Cousin and her Husband, did not take kindly to my Son. His endorsement would only discredit my First Cousin's Husband's proposal.

"All this is fine, but what are we to do?" I asked.

"Make a stand for Democracy!" he cried. "Hold Elections! Democratic Elections, this is the key, the acupuncture point, this is the nostril of the bull where you insert the ring, this is the central link of the chain! Everybody run for Elections! Let everyone make an election speech, like bidding for a contract: how much you charge, the kind of food you will supply, the obligations of the members of the family who join your program, how much you expect to get paid. Everything

must be Open, Transparent, Codified, Documented, Legal-
ized, Programmed, and Systemized. Let the Ballot decide!
Let the People cast their vote! Let the Majority rule! The mi-
nority must give in to the Majority. This principle in itself is
an indication of a new concept, new spirit, new order, offset-
ting Rigidity on the one hand, and Anarchism on the other!"

Father thought this over very carefully, the lines of
his forehead creasing even deeper as his thoughts were profound. Finally he said: "Yes, I am all for it. But there are two
obstacles to overcome. One is the Patriarch, he might object.
The other is Elder Sister Xu . . ."

First Cousin's Husband answered: "No problem as
far as the Patriarch is concerned. He rides with the times.
And anyway, he is sick and tired of overseeing the food. The
real problem is Elder Sister . . ."

Here my Son lost patience: "What is Elder Sister Xu
to us, and what are we to Elder Sister Xu? She is not a member of our family, she has no right to vote, anyway."

My Mother remonstrated: "My Grandson, did you
say that Elder Sister Xu has no right to vote? You don't know
what you are talking about. Elder Sister Xu might not share
our family name, might not be one of the clan. But let me tell
you, you won't get anything done unless you have her on
your side. I have been in this family my whole life, I should
know! What do you know?"

The camp of my First Cousin and her Husband was
split over this issue. My First Cousin's Husband held that
making a special case for Elder Sister Xu would be betraying
the principle of Democracy. Democracy and Special Considerations were mutually incompatible. My First Cousin retorted that it was very well to talk, but what was the use of
highfalutin talk if out of touch with reality? Belittling Elder
Sister Xu was as good as belittling Tradition, belittling Tradition would cost you your footing in reality, and without a

firm footing in reality, any project for reform was just day-dreaming, and a daydream reform was just hot air. My First Cousin did not stand on ceremony with her Husband. She said outright: "Don't think you are somebody just because you have been over the seas and can say a few foreign words! Actually in our family, you are not worth Elder Sister Xu's little finger!"

At these words, My First Cousin's Husband paled, smiled aloofly, and walked out of the room.

A few days later, Uncle tried to patch things up and find a solution. He pointed out that the so-called two obstacles were but one, that Elder Sister Xu may have been a diehard Conservative, but she always listened to Grandfather. If Grandfather gives the nod, so will she. There was no basis for the conflict between the democratic Process and Elder Sister Xu's special case, even less reason to bring such an imaginary conflict to a crisis.

Uncle's words dispelled the clouds. Everything seemed so clear. All our worries were much ado about nothing. All this hassle over conflicting views and such, it was really in the eye of the beholder: now it's there, and then it's gone, now it's looming, and then it's shrinking. The real test is how to find a common ground for different opinions, so as to create a relaxed, friendly, and trustful atmosphere. We were all much elated and full of confidence. Even my First Cousin's Husband and my Son couldn't help smiling with relief.

We unanimously entrusted Uncle and Father with the task of winning over Elder Sister Xu. Just as Uncle had predicted, it was smooth sailing all the way. True, Elder Sister was stoutly opposed to elections. "A lot of fuss and bother over nothing!" she snorted. But she also announced that having gotten safely out of this last illness she had retreated from all worldly contention. She supported nothing, opposed nothing. "If you want to lunch on flies, I'll eat flies. If you want to dine on mosquitoes, I'll eat mosquitoes. Just don't ask me about anything." She didn't even care whether or not she had the Right to Vote. She declared that she had nothing to say on any issue and would not join in on the family discussions. To all intents and purposes, Elder Sister Xu had faded from the historical stage.

We all elected the Husband of my First Cousin to be in charge of the election. What with a general housecleaning, and wiping of windowpanes, and hanging up of calligraphy scrolls, and setting out vases of the latest design of plastic flowers, the approaching date for the election actually brought a festive atmosphere. Democracy brings change, there's no denying it. The day finally arrived. My First Cousin's Husband directed the operation. He wore his overseas gray suit and black tie, like a conductor at a concert. For a beginning, he requested that each of us make a campaign speech on the topic "My Program to Run the Household."

Nobody spoke. One could hear the flies buzzing. My First Cousin's Husband asked: "What? No one running? I thought you were all full of ideas!"

I said: "Cousin, why don't you begin and set an example? You see, we are not used to Democracy. Quite embarrassing, really."

His Wife, my First Cousin, butted in: "Certainly not. What has it to do with him?"

My First Cousin's Husband explained in a quiet, gentlemanly manner: "I am not running for election. It was not for my personal interest that I brought up the idea of Democracy. Now if you elected me, that would discredit the idea of Democracy! And anyway, I am applying for studies abroad. I am in touch with several institutions in North America and Oceania. Once I have bought enough foreign currency on the black market, I will leave. If anyone in present company volunteers to help me out a little, I'd be grateful. I'm borrowing in RMB and repaying in foreign currency . . ."[5]

We looked at each other, completely flabbergasted. It occurred to us in a flash that this Election gadget was just asking for trouble! Wasn't it a trap, too, this speechifying, making promises right and left? Such lack of respect for one's ancestors. So inconsiderate to one's neighbors. And anyway, how can you please everybody if you were elected to run the household? There must be a screw loose somewhere, not leaving well enough alone, but playing with Elections! It occurred to us then and there that we had eaten our porridge and pickles and bean-curd paste noodles for the last several decades without Democratic Elections, and we had done just fine. Without Democratic Elections, we had neither starved nor burst with food, we had neither gnawed at bricks nor drank dog's piss by mistake, nor had we sipped our noodles into our nostrils or up our asses. But now we have to meddle in this wretched Democracy, ending up with diarrhea on the one hand and starvation on the other! This is the Chinese for you. We won't leave well enough alone until we had got everybody bloated with edema.[6]

But then it occurred to us that since we had already made a commitment to Democracy, we might as well enjoy a taste of it. Since the stage was set for Elections, we might as well have a go at it. Since we were all gathered together, especially since the Patriarch has put in an appearance, the show should go on. And anyway, why should we write off Democratic Elections without giving it a chance? Supposing it works? Supposing Democratic Elections would result in

5. A satirical allusion to overseas language class enrollment with foreign currency bought on the black market.
6. An allusion to the Great Leap Forward, which caused widespread urban edema and famine in rural areas.

good food, tasty and healthy, comprising all the requirements of smell, taste, and color, nurturing the yin and ener-
gizing the yang, reviving the blood and instilling vital energy, strengthening the constitution while keeping the body
in shape; supposing it could save grocery bills and conserve
energy, meet sanitary requirements without bureaucracy, re-
duce smoke and muffle noise; supposing everybody could
have a say without having to rack their brains, and someone
were in charge but without having the last word; supposing
nobody had to eat leftovers yet all waste avoided, and oys-
ters could be had without hepatitis and seafood without the
fishy smell; supposing Democratic Elections could bring
these benefits, only a fool would not have a go at it.

So the Election took place: filling in the ballots, putting them into the ballot box, supervising the opening of the
box, counting the ballots. Eleven ballot forms were handed
out, eleven retrieved. Thus, the Election was declared valid.
Of the ballot forms retrieved, four were blank, that is to say,
no candidate's name was filled in. One came up with "anybody will do" which was as good as void. Of the rest, there
were two votes for Elder Sister Xu, three votes for Grandfather, and one vote for my Son.

Grandfather had the most votes, but not the required
majority. It was not half, not even one-third of the votes.
What was to be done? Was he elected? We had not thought of
that beforehand. We sought out my First Cousin's Husband
for enlightenment. My First Cousin's Husband said there
were two kinds of "laws" in the world, one documented, the
other undocumented. Strictly speaking, undocumented laws
were not binding. For instance, he explained, the limit on the
number of presidential terms was not written in the U.S.
Constitution, and was not law in the strict sense of the word.
It was just a convention. The basic concept of Democracy, according to him, was majority rule. But what was a major-

30

ity? Wasn't majority relative? What is a Simple Majority?—anything more than half? What is an Absolute Majority?—anything over two-thirds? It all depends on tradition, and working concepts. As to our Election, he said, since it was our first try, and since we were all flesh-and-blood family members, it was up to us to decide.

Here my First Cousin barged in and announced that since Grandfather had the most votes he was elected. She assured us that this was not a case of Feudal Authoritarianism, but the workings of a Modern Democracy. She added further that there was no danger of Patriarchal Authoritarianism in our family anyway, much less that it would constitute the Main Contradition and the Main Danger. According to her, on the contrary, we should be wary of Anarchism under the guise of so-called Anti-Feudalism, and steer clear of Liberalism, Self-Centeredness, Subjectivism, Overconsumption, Epicureanism, and the Blind Worship of Things Foreign, like the fallacy that the moon over the U.S. is rounder than it is over China, and other such foreign dogmas.[7]

Here my Son suddenly got all worked up and announced in no uncertain terms that he had not cast the vote for himself. As he said it, all eyes were turned on me, as if I had cast the vote for him, as if I was guilty of the dishonorable practice of voting for my own flesh and blood. I blushed in spite of myself. Then I asked myself, who would think so, and why should they think so? Did it occur to them that even if I had voted for my Son it would not comprise any offense, because in not voting for my Son, I could only have chosen among My Father, My Mother, My Wife, My First Cousin, and so on. And anyway, according to the currently fashionable Freudian theories, would my First Cousin necessarily be

7. An allusion to the controversy over the "main danger": "feudal" trends, or "capitalist" trends.

31

more removed from me than my own Son? After all, my Son might be suffering from an Oedipus Complex and harboring plans to kill me and marry my Wife. Had they thought of that? Why should they point the accusing finger at me the minute my Son made a move?

By now, my Son was shouting at the top of his voice. He said the fact that he had one vote meant that the voice of humanity was not completely stifled, that the torch was still alight and would one day burst into a prairie fire. He said that he had concerned himself with the Reform of the family Menu purely in a spirit of giving, out of respect for the humanist tradition and an all-encompassing Love. Coming to the word Love, tears as big as soy beans dropped from his eyes. He said there was order in the family but no Love, and order without Love, like marriage without Love, was immoral. He said that he could have detached himself from our familial eating system long ago and gone his own way and dined on snails and cheese and asparagus and tuna fish and shrimps and veal and Kentucky Fried Chicken and sandwiches and Big Macs and apple pie and vanilla pudding. He also added that he loved his Aunt, meaning my First Cousin, but that he found Aunt's views unacceptable, no matter how enticing they might sound to the ears.

At this point Uncle put in a word. Note that he did not interrupt, that would have been rude. But to put in a word denotes intimacy and wisdom and a spirit of Democracy; in a word, it was conferring an honor on the speaker. Uncle began by saying that my First Cousin's wording of the Main Contradiction and the Main Danger was not in keeping with the official wording on the issue. He himself felt it advisable never to emphasize any one aspect of a problem as the Main Danger. According to his own lifetime experience as a practicing physician, he said, the minute you pinpointed constipation as the Main Danger, it was bound to end in universal diarrhea, leading to a sellout of all pills for diarrhea and distrust of doctors in general. On the other hand, if you pointed to diarrhea as the Main Danger, it was bound to end in universal constipation leading to hernia, with the additional problem of pent-up energies building into a "Heat Syndrome" and breaking out in fistfights. The pent-up energies are fanned by fire, and the fire must be quelled by water. Only when the five elements are balanced can one maintain good health. Thus, concluded Uncle, one must be on guard against diarrhea on the one hand, and constipation on the other. Deal with the one or the other as they come. It is best, of course, to be neither constipated nor suffering from diarrhea. As Uncle finished, I thought I heard the sound of clapping.

After the clapping, we discovered that our problem was still there. Moreover, our metabolism seems to have been hastened by all this discussion of the five elements. Anyway, we were hungry. So we decided that as Grandfather had the most votes, he should be in charge.

Grandfather did not agree. He said that cooking was a technical issue. It had nothing to do with politics, ideology, seniority, status, power, privilege, or one's place in the hierarchy. He said what we needed to elect was not the best leader but the best cook. Nothing else but skill at stewing and stir-fry were the required qualifications.

My son applauded, and everybody felt this was truly an original line of thinking, a new breakthrough. But some pointed out that time was short, that they were hungry. The fact was that, although the search for the right person to oversee our household menu was still in the stage of discussion, when the hour came round we all wanted our dinner. The discussion might have results, or the discussion could end in nothing, but we all wanted our dinner. Some might agree with the decision arrived at in the discussion, and some might not, but we all wanted our dinner. With permission, we wanted our dinner. Without permission we wanted it just the same. And so, we went our several ways to feed our bellies.

Setting up the cooking competition was quite complicated. The requirements were that we each had to make one batch of steamed bread, one pot of rice, two scrambled eggs, a platter of chopped pickled turnips, one bowl of thin porridge, and one stewed rump of pork. To work out this program, we had altogether spent thirty days and thirty nights in discussion. There had been tension, arguments, quarrels, tears, and reconciliations. By the end, we were so exhausted that we could hardly make water or walk on our own two legs. The overall result was that we had hurt each others' feelings, but had also exchanged views, that we had exhausted ourselves, but also had a lot of fun. When the question of the two scrambled eggs was brought up, we tumbled over each other with laughter as if we shared a secret joke. When the requirement for chopping pickled turnips was brought up, the whole company was downcast, as if we had suddenly aged. To make a long story short, the cooking skill competition took place and the results were released. The grading went very smoothly; nobody raised any objections. The results were thus:

First Class First Grade: Grandfather and Grandmother.

First Class Second Grade: Father, Mother, Uncle, Aunt.

Second Class First Grade: I, my Wife, my First Cousin, my First Cousin's Husband.

Third Class First Grade: my Son.

We were then concerned that my Son, only getting Third Class, might be hurt, so we decided to give him a certificate of Special Honor, the "Star of Hope" Certificate. Of course it goes without saying that he was still Third Class in spite of being "Star of Hope." Anyway, theories and terms and methodology may vary, but order was invariable.

Time passed. People were vaguely aware that all things in heaven and earth find their own balance. So after a while, our fever of excitement over the great eating debate fizzled out, and the heat of controversy over theory and terms and methodology and experimentation gradually cooled down. We did not rack our brains over whether it was a technical problem or a cultural issue, a question of institutional structure or something never dreamt of in our philosophy. We stopped racking our brains over the problem. It seemed that without solving these knotty questions, we still managed to feed our bellies.

Elder Sister Xu passed away peacefully. She lay down for her afternoon nap and never woke up. We all remember her, respect her, and venerate her memory. My Son went to work for a joint-venture company. He has probably realized his target of bread and butter daily with mounds of animal fat. On holidays back home, he would say that he had had his fill of rich foods and now only hankered after porridge and pickles, thin soup, and bean-curd paste noodles, adding in a shamefaced sort of way: "Concepts change easily, but the palate is stubborn."

Now, Uncle and Aunt have moved into their own apartment in a new building and do their own cooking. They have a brand new kitchen with pipe gas and an exhaust fan. They have tried stewed rump and they have tried scrambled eggs, but they still cannot do without sliced steamed bread, thin porridge, pickled turnips, thin soup, and bean-curd paste noodles. Our First Cousin's Husband finally made it abroad for "further studies," studying and working at the same time, and his wife joined him later. He writes: "Here, our favorite food is porridge and pickles. Picking up our bowl of porridge with pickles, we feel as if we were back in home sweet home, and for the moment forget that we are wanderers in a strange land. It can't be helped, it seems that porridge and pickles are in our genes."

I stay with Father and Grandfather and we live happily ever after. We eat much more meat and chicken and fish and milk and sugar and fat than ever before. We have all put on weight. Our table is groaning under dishes of fancy cooking in ever-changing rounds of novelties. We had stir-fried pork and we had sea slugs, we had fried peanuts and we had cream pastry, we had cold bean-curd skin and we had shrimp salad. We even had abalone and scallops on one occasion. The abalone and the sea slugs came and went, the salad was eaten and forgotten. But thin porridge and pickles outlasted them all. Even after a gourmet feast of all the delicacies extracted from seas and mountains, we still have to sit down to a dessert of porridge and pickles. Only with porridge and pickles as a base can our digestive organs—esophagus, stomach, intestines, liver, spleen, and gall bladder—operate normally. Without this last touch of thin porridge and pickles, stomachache and gas would immediately attack us, and who knows what else, perhaps even cancer. Thanks to porridge and pickles, we have so far been preserved from stomach or intestinal cancer. I can state that porridge and pickles make up the Headrope in the Net System of our Eating; the gourmet dishes are only subsidiaries, the Meshes of the Net. Only when the Headrope is pulled up can all the Meshes open out.[8]

Since Elder Sister Xu's death, Mother now shoulders the Momentous Task of cooking. According to rote, Mother

8. An allusion to late Chairman Mao Zedong's famous dictum: "Class struggle is the headrope. Only when the headrope [of a fishing net] is pulled out do all the meshes open."

36

would ask Grandfather and Grandmother: "Soup, or no soup? Pork—shredded, or sliced?" The faithful repetition of this ancient query was soothing to the heart, an expression of a moral sentiment, a dedication to the memory of Elder Sister Xu. Her spirit seems to come alive in the observance of this seemingly empty ritual of question and answer. Grandfather finally announced that so long as there was porridge and pickles, toasted slices of steamed bread and bean-curd paste noodles, all the rest was immaterial and would be left to Mother's own discretion. He begged Mother not to challenge him with all sorts of knotty questions. Mother answered submissively and did as she was told, but always felt something was missing if she didn't ask first. When the food was on the table, she would peer around apprehensively, carefully studying Grandfather's face for any signs of disaffection. If Grandfather coughed, she would say softly to herself that perhaps there had been a speck of sand in the rice. Perhaps the pickles had been too salty. Or too bland. She would thus murmur to herself, not daring to ask outright. Of course, even if she had asked Grandfather from the beginning, there might still be specks of sand in the rice.

One of these days, Mother is bound to pick up her courage again and go to Grandfather, asking most submissively, conscious that she is bothering Grandfather against his injunctions: "Pork—sliced, or shredded?" And Grandfather's tone as he answered would be benevolent even in firmness. Even if it was only to say, "Do not ask me," it would still be a sort of answer. And then Mother, her mind set at ease, would go back to finish her cooking.

A friend from England came for a visit, a friend of Father's from the forties. He stayed with us for a week. We went out of our way to hire a Western-style chef to make steak and pastry for him but he said: "Frankly, I am not here to eat this nondescript mess that you take to be Western food.

Please give me something at once traditional and unique. Please!" What could we do? We had no choice but to give him thin porridge and pickles.

"What simplicity! What elegance! How tender! How soothing! Where else but in the mysterious Orient can one meet with this kind of elixir!" I taped his rhapsody of thin porridge in an impeccable Oxford accent, and played the cassette to my Son.

The Wind on the Plateau

What is the greatest felicity for a sentient creature in a city in China in the eighties of the twentieth century? A bonus? The meager ones everyone gets have long been regarded as a right that no one would feel much compunction about accepting one four times greater as his due. A huge bonus? But where are they to be had? Promotion? Of the few who contemplate setting foot on the ladder, fewer still have the monomania of the true craver after official posts. Winning a lottery? The one-time tickets were sold for an international marathon in the capital, the police were dispatched in force, and people were almost crushed to death, when the chance of winning was one in 49,999. An understanding spouse? When one is young, perhaps, and even then, despite the ubiquity of ridiculously immoral and loveless marriages, the overall matrimonial tendency is not the desire for a lover. All young men love, as do all young women, and an obscure natural law decrees that the proportion of the one to the other is about equal and that no more than three percent of the marriageable population remain unmarried, thus guaranteeing there be no threat to the prosperity of the country. Vicissitudes have proved the proportion safe.

No, the single most wonderful thing that has happened to quite large numbers of people in recent years is to be given a new apartment. To know the joy that this gives, one has only to see the wretchedness of those with inadequate housing; and to know the importance of allotting the housing one need only see how those in charge calculate as finely as a general confronting a dangerous enemy and how the applicants marshal all their prestige, words, and brains. The yearly toll of gray hairs acquired in both pursuits is not low.

Thus it was that early in 1984 for Song Chaoyi of Dongquan City to be given two apatments was no small matter but the consummation of everything good which he had experienced since the winter of 1978. It was a minor high tide. On January 14, after much wrangling and rushing about, many clashes, excuses, false alarms, a showdown, waiting, despair, and hope rekindled, he received six keys, three for each apartment. The grooved keys of aluminum alloy looked like any other keys, still smelling of dust and dirty with their protective coating of oil. He was pleased to get them, but not as happy as he had expected to be.

After work he pushed his way onto a bus. The winter wind cut his face through the open windows and the smoked chicken in one passenger's string bag seemed to keep pecking at his thigh, but being a man experienced in the hardships of life, there was happiness mingled with his annoyance, for nowadays chickens cooked in many ways were to be had everywhere; they went well with wine, and if the house had central heating—

That would be even better. He waited forty-three minutes to change to a No. 2. Maybe there had been an accident somewhere along the route. They were more common in winter when everybody was encumbered with heavy padded clothes. Actually, he needed to go only three stops and could make it in twenty minutes on foot, yet he decided to wait, the more stubbornly the longer he waited, while the skin of his face seemed to freeze to a crisp crust and give him a better view of things, as he recalled how he had wet his pants in the freezing cold as a boy and how during the "cultural revolution" the cold had made him throw up the sorghum he had just swallowed, his only source of energy.

He got home at seven forty-four. Slowly, he produced the keys. His wife and son jumped for joy. These are for you. And he seemed to see a vision of flowers, stone steps, easy chairs, and a spectrum of colored lights flashing beautiful patterns. He felt a comfortable glow at the thought of the ramshackle farmhouse they had lived in for so many years, and though he was exhausted when supper was over at half past eight, his wife and son insisted on setting out to inspect the apartments, as if they would fly away if it were put off for a single day. Possession of the keys had banished all patience. They changed buses twice and were there in fifty-two minutes. Carefully they mounted the dim, narrow, twisting stairs; softly they turned the key, opened the door, and turned on the light. The walls were all white, and their faces were no less pale.

Moving was a joyous occasion that left memories like the scenes in a television series, long-winded, tiring, flawed, and dubious but still enough to keep you away from work so as to follow every episode.

His son's friends helped them move, clocking up twenty-four man-journeys, and to reward them he bought, through a supply manager for the People's Political Consultative Conference, twenty-four bottles of beer, two bottles of liquor, and vast quantities of ham, sausage, fried fish and shrimps, and pigs' trotters stewed the color of red roses. The lower part of the bathroom wall was sanded and painted light green with materials and labor obtained through the good offices of a school friend he had not seen for twenty-five years and whom he thanked with a banquet at the Loushanglou Restaurant, a meal whose quality was ensured by the intervention of another school friend he had had no contact with for twenty-four years.

Getting a gas cylinder he broke the record. A clerk at the Dongquan Gas Company told him that this would be no easier than getting the housing, so of course a letter of recommendation had to be written, not by the school where he worked but by the Municipal Standing Committee of the People's Congress and the Consultative Conference. It began: "Representative to the National People's Congress, Vice-chairman of the Municipal People's Political Consultative Conference, Vice-chairman of the Association of Overseas Chinese, Vice-chairman of the Association of Social Science Workers, and relation of overseas Chinese Comrade Song Chaoyi needs a gas cylinder." His great titles ran to several lines of narrow-spaced small type, including the redundancy about being a relative of overseas Chinese and Vice-chairman of the Association of Overseas Chinese while omitting all mention of his job as a teacher. He was of two minds as to whether his status as a relation of overseas Chinese would prove to be the clinching factor or a signal embarrassment, but as it turned out the uncle of a schoolmate of his son's girlfriend got the cylinder for him in merely a week.

The new housing of Song Chaoyi consisted of two apartments, the larger of which had three rooms and a hall, a balcony at the front and one at the back, a kitchen, and a bathroom, while the smaller comprised one room, a hall, a balcony, a kitchen, and a bathroom. The latter was essentially used by his son except for the kitchen, which was converted into a storeroom for the family's books and papers. The three rooms in the larger apartment became a bedroom, sitting room, and workroom. In the hall were a plastic-topped, chrome-legged table, convertible at need into a round dining table, and some soft, springy folding chairs with similarly shiny chrome legs, these last doubling as dining chairs and seating for other guests. Life went up a rung. Song sauntered from one apartment to the other, looking at the bookcase in this one and opening the desk drawers in that, as curious and fascinated as entering the formal set of a television program.

Over the past five years, strokes of luck had arrived like an intermittent stream of goldfish. There had been exoneration, the move back to town from the countryside, the appointment as a special top-grade teacher, three increments in salary at once, and the publication of a thousand copies in hardcover of his book on the rural teaching of Chinese. His sister—the overseas Chinese who enabled him to be the relation of an overseas Chinese—had visited twice with her foreign husband, whom after an initial feeling of discomfort Song had discovered to be quite important. And at the same time he got the apartments, he sent him money, which brought him foreign exchange certificates and overseas Chinese coupons. All this seemed to have given wings to a tiger. His son, abetted by his wife, set busily about fixing up the new apartments, so much so that the string in Song's heart which was attuned to poverty frequently quivered as if his favorite piece of porcelain had shattered when he surveyed the objects occupying the space of his home: the magnificent refrigerator, the television set, the radio—cassette recorder, the easy chairs, the modern furniture, and the spring beds.

He was fifty-four, and for fifty-four years he had lived cramped and shabbily, out at the elbows and on tenterhooks, though this adverse environment had made him peculiarly kind, innocent, and carefree. It was a life he was accustomed to just as a dutiful son is accustomed to looking after a bedridden mother who is incorrigibly moody but nevertheless his mother toward whom he owes gratitude. As compensation for leaving this mother he has known since birth, not even the three-door Hitachi refrigerator and the Sharp stereo could quite overcome his impression of weightlessness and loss, sensations that science claims to be beneficial but to which few can adjust.

He wondered if happiness were not mainly something for others to see, a display sample rather than a thing enjoyable in itself.

Callers at the new home, whether old friends, new friends, old contacts, or new contacts, were unstinting in their praise:

All the eight modern conveniences, I see. No need for you to wait for the year 2000!

So this is what they mean by getting rich first!

You'll be seeing the good times at last, then!

It's worlds away from what you had before, I must say!

You know, one could *die* content in a flat like this!

The last comment jarred on Song's ears. What, die? To be born in trouble and die in comfort? Well, the ancients always linked comfort with death.

The person who had said this had been his best friend, Zhao, who stood one meter ninety and whose father had been extremely wealthy and high-ranking at the time of the Northern Expedition. Zhao had many hobbies and many accomplishments. He could play music and chess, paint and do calligraphy, take photographs, sing Beijing opera and *dagu*, and stand on his head, not to mention plaster and build stoves. In none of these things was he skilled. His life had improved a good deal in the past few years, but he still wore the same down-and-out appearance, with his chin unshaved, his hair uncombed, and his collar unbuttoned, and his every utterance was tinged with misfortune.

Could it be true? Does death equal peace? And does living then mean struggling with gritted teeth, taking one blow after another? He had seen a film when he was still young called *The Mexican*. The Mexican had borne in silence the blows that rained down on his head, face, and chest. He had walked up the springboard with a sack on his back so heavy he felt as if the addition of one straw would have broken his back. As for himself, in a cold classroom that let in the four winds he had imparted the true meaning of life to children sitting on earthen bricks so that they should live better lives in the future. He had baked a piece of red sweet potato for his son. He had read beside a kerosene lamp, rubbing watery eyes. Poor as he had been, he still tried to save and had had a hundred yuan in a savings account. To live meant tenacity.

Now every morning he thoroughly washed the mop under the tap and wiped the concrete floor until it shone as if with wax polish, and the new concrete had a pleasant alkaline smell. The sun streamed in through white lace curtains onto the green narcissus leaves. On the wall was a painting of horses by Xu Beihong. The Oscar-winning theme song of *Love Story* was often to be heard from his stereo, the low notes of the cello warm and solemn. His guests, seated in cushioned easy chairs, were offered Double Happiness cigarettes and drank tea that cost one yuan seventy an ounce. After their departure he adjusted the elegant upholstery and, like a survivor of an air crash arriving home or a marathon runner soaking in a hot bath after the race, closed his eyes and sighed with relief.

Yet he felt a certain unease. His colleagues and friends did not live such easy lives. One influential newspaper had reported on its front page that a school on the outskirts of Baoding had a principal with the "big monthly salary" of a hundred and twenty yuan, and the same article had pointed out that a common laborer in the nearby countryside earned a hundred or so a month, a hundred and thirty or forty if skilled. If this was the improved salary of a primary or middle school principal, what must the teachers be getting? The Pinghe District Education Bureau had said that for the first time in thirty years it had a few apartments for local teachers, provided that both husband and wife had worked for five years in the district and lived in accommodations with less than 2.5 square meters a head. He felt like hanging himself.

His son meanwhile was going in and out of the apartments with head held high as if they were his and his father was merely a lodger. Ten centimeters taller than his father, Longlong was a chip off the old block, only smarter, as hand on hip he inspected the apartments, laid plans, organized purchases, moved and decorated, all with a smile of proud derision that ignored his father's overwhelming reverence and awe.

Song did not like his son's attitude. Setbacks should not be forgotten when times are good. Always bear in mind that not a thread of clothing nor a grain of food is easily come by. Take nothing for granted. How much jollier the boy had been helping him dig a cellar and make mud bricks on the farm, birdsnesting and playing games with the country boys.

Song's few passable friends had been more comfortable and their houses had been better than his own. In recent years as Song's situation had, albeit amid apprehension and trepidation, improved, culminating in this wonderful accommodation, they had ceased to visit him and sent fewer invitations, a change he had failed to notice, continuing to call on them, smoking, drinking tea, and cracking melon seeds in their homes with every intention of staying for supper, though he was never asked to do so, and the way they treated him—even looked at him—was not as it had been.

At the same time, a large number of new people had begun to visit him, leaders and subordinates at the places that had given him titles and a variety of people from other cities and countries. One announced himself as general manager of National Correspondence Teaching. Others again came to admire and reminisce. Like a tape recorder, he repeated his place of birth, age, résumé, marital status, number of children, salary bracket, official and sideline work, and so on. His new friends were puzzled that he still worked in a middle school, a situation they found illogical and irrational. These people, who felt like old friends on first meeting, sincerely suggested that he get himself transferred to the United Front or the Department of Overseas Chinese or some office dealing with foreign affairs, for to them being a schoolteacher was socially the dregs.

But that's my vocation. That's where everything else comes from.

Of course, his new friends hinted, but you have many things other don't, so it's not important to go on teaching. In fact it may well work against you, because the less actual teaching you do, the more it proves how well, how superbly, how incomparably you *used* to teach. No, really: the top grades, the authorities, don't work, or they are unable to work. What else is the point of being a special top-grade teacher?

There just seemed to be some sort of grand design in it.

A leader of the municipal party committee had tried to talk him into a transfer to the Overseas Chinese Affairs Office. He had refused, remembering the grand design. Some had said he did right. Others had called him a fool who had gotten into small-time habits from working so long in the countryside. Still others had ascribed to him the cunning of the man of great wisdom who likes to appear slow-witted.

However, Overseas Chinese Affairs Office or no, he became busier than ever and began to notice, between his busy moments, that his wife, Jiang Chun, was looking aggrieved.

"What's the matter with you?" he asked.

"Oh, nothing," she replied despondently.

"I don't know, I suppose, well, I've been too busy lately to go to the movies with you, or to the park, or shopping."

"Why take me? Surely I'd just be a burden," she said coldly.

It was a bolt from the blue to the straightforward, hardworking Song, who was so much in love with his wife that he had told her that he had not dared to love her at first, but that when he thought that if he didn't marry her, no one in her life would love her as much, he had realized the enormity of the crime of not marrying her. He had believed it. He still did. What had he done to upset her?

"Is it something I've done?" He spoke softly, trying to stay calm and patient. "Somehow you seem recently . . ."

She was small and slim, nearing fifty, though she still looked like a girl from behind. One know-it-all claimed that Jiang had trained as an actress, for without a cultural interest how could she possibly have picked Song in his difficult days and calmly and persistently stuck to him through it all?

"It's nothing," she said, her expression belying her words.

"It must be something. Tell me. Don't hide it from me. What has made you unhappy? Is it your work? Your life? The apartments? Is it me?"

"My work, my life, the apartments, and you are all fine. I'm the happiest person on earth."

It was her cynicism that finally infuriated him. "Just what is it I've done? I've worked hard, I've had no time to myself. I've been through hard times, I've been insulted, I've been wronged, and now when life's improving and we've got such good apartments—wasn't it you who encouraged me to get them?"

48

"Forget it, forget it." Jiang waved her hand and, standing on tiptoe, put a hand over his mouth. A forced, bitter smile crossed her face.

Tears welled up in her eyes. She looked away from Song. What was she looking at?

The eyes of his son were often just as unfathomable. He slept in every day in his little apartment. He read Laozi and Kant, traditional Chinese pharmacology and Hugo and spoke cynically of his director's speeches and popular fiction. He listened to black spirituals, rejecting his father's suggestion that he listen to Beethoven's *Ninth*. When he watched television he changed channels and adjusted the antenna with a frequency that made it impossible to follow any program properly. In his eyes one saw frivolity, grief, and skepticism. His knowledge was shallow, his aspirations great. If he did not belong to the collapsed generation, he was certainly one of the perplexed.

They lack the enthusiastic dedication of our generation, thought Song, beginning to be worried about the future of the country.

Anyway, women were always a puzzle.

And so was the younger generation, with its incomprehensible addiction to wildly howling spirituals.

It was fate. In the first half of his life he had tried to change himself and conform to what society expected, in his smoking habits, the tone he adopted, even in the way he walked. To discard the image of a bastard of the exploiting class he never bought cigarettes that cost more than fifteen cents. Naturally endowed with a resonant, clear, precise voice, he sometimes, in order to fit in in the countryside, affected a tongue-tied, faltering manner of speech, purposely jumbling his words, dropping sentences and stuttering. He hunched his back and bowed his head as he walked to show humility instead of conceit. He even, quite heartlessly, broke with his sister who lived abroad. But in the end the blows had rained down as they had on the face of the Mexican.

But life had in the past few years initiated the common saying he hated most by "springing up like sesame flowers." Teaching Chinese for years had given him a distaste for, a prejudice against, this unbearably vulgar turn of phrase whose pretended evocativeness was to him mere garrulity, yet it occurred to him whenever he thought of the recent improvements in his life. Such retribution!

And when even his sister had turned out to be a cause of the turn in his luck, the sister who resolutely opposed communism, who had refused to return to China and had gone instead to Taiwan and then to the United States and married a white man—he was so ashamed that he could gladly have burrowed into the ground.

The apartments were a puzzle too. At college, he had quoted Marx's *Das Kapital* to prove that the dormitory, where students slept in two-tier bunks, compared unfavorably with the workshops of nineteenth-century Britain for neglect of the workers. For this he had been criticized as a "wielder of the red flag against the red flag," thus becoming an "element," who had to share a small room with sixteen others, all sleeping on the ground so jammed together that they had to turn over at the same time. But he had slept soundly then.

Before his present move they had shared a courtyard with eight others. They seemed to live under one roof. It was not uncommon for pickles to be fermenting in the room or for a grown son to be separated from his parents by a suspended bedsheet. When he could not see his neighbors, he still had been able to hear their voices and the chiming of their clocks; when they ate chilies his eyes had smarted with theirs, owing it seemed to the commodious passageways afforded by the cracked and unplastered upper partitions between.

He tossed and turned in the new apartment. Was it too quiet? Was he too busy? Was it too comfortable? Did it smell too bland? Was he going through male menopause? It seemed to lack something weighty, something that tied you down.

Awake, he often recalled his early days after his reacceptance by Dongquan, when they had been temporarily accommodated in the narrow, dingy storeroom of a small, sixth-grade hotel. The table, chairs, stools, and boxes of wood and rattan that they had brought back from their cold northerly village had been far too much for the six square meters provided and had had to be stored at the Education Bureau to be eaten by mice. The dim little room, opposite the public washroom, had regaled them with the sounds of guests washing their faces, brushing their teeth, blowing their noses, and spitting and of attendants swilling their spittoons and mops. The room had backed onto the shed containing the only television set, which had deafened them nightly with the din of gongs, drums, and loud shouting, the size of the audience requiring the set to be turned up as loud as was possible. But the excitement with which he and Jiang—their son had not returned with them—had moved into that room after their long wait! It had been their reward for years of injustice and hibernation. Everything had been coming alive again, resuscitating, the glacier melting, the trees blossoming, their own lives and souls, still imbued, whatever anyone said, with the lofty sentiments of the old, singing to the new era. He and Jiang had visited old friends together and together had walked along every street and lane that they had frequented in their young days and had not seen for so long, rejoicing and shedding tears at every crossroads, corner, lamp, and at all the houses old and new. It had been a magic little room, its confines bursting with happiness, its dimness radiant with hope.

What had happened? He had reacquired all his skill with remarkable speed, his wide knowledge and good memory, his analogical reasoning, his flexibility and superb presentation, and added to them a fervor for work and service which exploded after long years of suppression. Refusing the well-meant suggestion of a job in the Education Bureau, he had taught. He had studied hard, written, and taught, shaking all of Dongquan and the province with a few demonstration classes and a book. From then on everything had been effortlessly smooth-going, and becoming representative of this organization and vice-chairman of that had seemed to make him teach even better. Even the inspector from Beijing had had nothing but praises for him after attending one class. Not a single suggestion for improvement in a fifteen-minute lecture. Nothing but praises.

In class, familiarity with his text made him sublime. A master of content, progression, and rhythm, precise as a computer, he foresaw and controlled his every action, word, laugh, turn of phrase, and tone of voice so as to coordinate them perfectly with the mood of his students. A smile, a conundrum, an intrigue, a sudden insight, a laugh, an exhilaration—all occurred where they should and to the degree required, so that the students were entirely won over in wholehearted admiration. Time flew by in his classes, which he ended punctually while the students still wanted more and he himself was fresher than when he had begun. It was true proficiency of art, an artistic selfishness and immateriality.

He was faultless, as faultless as a butcher cutting an ox, doing his job skillfully and with ease.

Probably it was just this faultlessness that was so dreadful. Zhao had linked his new apartments with death, and perhaps they were too perfect.

Yet his son was far from satisfied with things as they

were. He wanted video equipment, a musical door chime, a motorcycle, and a rubber dinghy. Why not go out and get an air conditioner made in Australia?

What about the cost? Six or seven thousand. And in electricity bills? A hundred or so a month. Song trembled with fury, while his son ridiculed him for a small-fry who knew nothing but to put his money in a pot and let it sleep. Didn't he know consumption brought turnover and turnover increased production?

Song wanted to box his ears for him, which while not effective enough to match the tide of *new thinking* would at least stave it off a bit.

Were his skill and his faultless teaching devolving into a retrograde pattern? His social commitments were so many that he sometimes had to get colleagues to mark his papers and coach his students. Was this the way to progress?

A young woman named Li had come to his school to teach the lower forms and made the first year hold a debate in her Chinese class. The discussion had become heated, and a girl not above one meter fifty tall had voiced doubts about a well-known essay by Lu Xun in the textbook. This had been called contentious. To question Lu Xun was ignorance, and the absurd behavior of Li and her undersized student had been censured by all the older teachers. It happened to be a time when capitalist liberalization was a bogey-word in art and literature, so that Li's experiment had been condemned as an expression of this vice, very much to the chagrin of special top-grade teacher Song.

His mortification was not on account of Li, whose setback was scarcely worth mentioning beside what he had undergone himself, but due rather to reflection that he himself needed only to preserve his rank of special top-grade teacher and not to start from scratch. Gone for him were the shudders, the groping, the new perils, the struggles, the misunderstanding, and the blame, for he was fifty-four, had made up for lost time in five short years, and was living a life that should have been his before. In Dongquan he could hardly surpass himself. He could no more imagine his teaching in 1982 being bettered by that in 1985, 1986, or 1987 than he could imagine improving his housing yet again this late in life. The saddest part was that he actually did teach well, to the point where asking him to do better was like asking Zhu Jianhua to jump higher when he had made 2.39 meters. And he could give Zhu Jianhua thirty years.

Happiness lies in hope or it is misfortune.

This is what he told the friend who had mentioned the contentment of dying in such an apartment. Zhao laughed, revealing teeth stained brown by cigarettes. You're letting it burn a hole in your pocket, do you know that? (In Hebei this old expression for the urge to squander had shifted its meaning to the uneasiness that banished enjoyment of an improved situation, just as the common people say that all misery is bearable but happiness is unenjoyable.) Didn't you explain in class how Fan Jin was so excited by winning the imperial examination that he went out of his mind with joy and had to be cuffed to his senses by his father-in-law till he threw up?[1] You really are letting it burn a hole. Suppose we change places and you let me have your apartments and your titles, okay?

He felt estranged and lonely at what Zhao had said. At night, as he opened his mail under the lamp, he was struck by the impression that the brighter the lamp the darker was the surrounding space. It was slowing down after the spurt that made him uneasy.

He lay in bed and after a succession of sighs confided in his wife.

1. An allusion to *The Scholars*, a classical Chinese novel satirical of scholars.

"I didn't reply when you asked me the other day why I was unhappy," she responded slowly. "But I was thinking that despite the better apartments, we—especially I—have lost so many precious things. Our youth, our hope for tomorrow, what we used to have when we were poor and hard up. The sympathy of our friends. Look critically at the people who come to see you now. They're either admiring and respectful or unctuous and wheedling. The ones who ask you to address meetings or accept titles or receive people are laughing up their sleeves all the time you're complaining of the burden of social pressure that affects your teaching, as if you were flaunting your greatness. So they coax you with 'people with ability should do more' and 'I know you're such a busy man but do try to make it.' Others are inspecting you and measuring you up. For all they're old friends, they scrutinize you as if you were a stranger, either because they're sorry for you or because they suspect you may drop them."

Song experienced a shock of enlightenment. "You're right. You're so right. You're the one with sharp eyes. It had never occurred to me."

"That's not the point," she went on, feeling the heat and easing her bare shoulders out of the quilt. "The problem is you. You're actually extremely conceited."

"You feel that way too, then?" He was stung.

Ignoring him, she continued. "Your eyes are smug but they're tired, they're busy but they're empty, they're relaxed but they're dull. Do you remember the time when we lived in that little hotel? When we mentioned our life and our work, your eyes used to shine like lamps."

"Did they?"

"And then there's me. Do you have time to think of me? Do you even remember my existence? You're busy, busy, busy. You have your profession, your engagements, your apartments. What do I have? We saw spring return together, and now you have your life to live."

"How can you say that? Doesn't everything I have belong to you?"

"Oh yes!" She laughted sardonically. "Everything I have is you and what you have, and everything you have is you and what you have too. What actually exists, what really exists, is what *you* have. Very generous of you to declare that everything you have belongs to me while I really have nothing but *you*." She sounded aggrieved and cynical.

Song, however, was losing his bearings. He had admired the perspicacity with which she had analyzed how they had lost their friends after moving, but he was at a loss to understand the way she talked about her own feelings, and the inability to fathom the meaning behind her hurt cynicism enraged him. "My work is tiring enough, but when I come home I hear not consolation but a maze of complaints! Shall we go back to the village, then? I have to agree with him now. This *is* letting it burn a hole."

Jiang, silenced as if by a sudden blow, tried hard not to sob, which only increased Song's annoyance. It was some time before she said softly to herself, "So you think that of me too. Twenty years ago I stopped seeing the boy my family had found for me and made up my mind to marry you. When I went to the countryside with you that's what they all said—father, mother, grandfather, my uncle, my cousin and her husband, and a fair number of my good friends too. They said I was letting it burn a hole in my pocket."

Song felt his heart flip over as if something precious had fallen into a well.

Waking at midnight, he heard the sound of wind, cars, distant voices, the mewing of cats, and the banging of windows. He wondered why he couldn't sleep. He went to the toilet, although he didn't need to, and noticed that his son's light was still on.

After they had moved, his sister, then on holiday in Rome, had written to him, saying, "You have had a hard time up till now. Do enjoy life."

The last words had been in English, as if she had had recourse to that language because the Chinese had no such notion or term. Translated, it became: make life happy.

Suddenly he understood Jiang. Life is suffering: when we cease suffering for it we suffer for ourselves. Oh my love!

At daybreak he set to work like a satellite entering orbit. Inertia and centripetal force govern healthy, normal movement. Was he really letting it burn a hole in his pocket?

He decided to go and see Li, who had been blamed for the teaching experiment. As he hadn't told her he was coming, he had to search for her address and made many inquiries in the twisting lanes before he found it, "the poor" who lived there knowing the place only by its old name.

He was shocked on his eventual arrival to discover that she lived with her family in a former gatehouse a foot below ground level. Entering it was like descending into a dim pit, but especially shocking were the three tiers of beds made by standing the feet of a two-tier set of bunks on six-inch piles of bricks. On the ground were spread a blanket and a quilt, and against the wall was a row of wooden and rattan boxes. On this level slept Li, thirty years old and unmarried.

She seemed surprised but happy to see him, made him tea and introduced him to her parents (who occupied the middle level) and her brother (who occupied the top). Her long, expressive eyes and the pleasantly vivacious smile that graced her admittedly pallid complexion, together with her slender figure and ringing voice, obliterated the humble nature of her abode and the awkwardness of her unmarried state. She seemed to Song to have more self-confidence than he did.

"Teaching methods can and should be approached from different angles. Don't mind what the others say. You mustn't take it to heart."

"I don't," she smiled, "not in the least."

Song nodded, feeling that he had poked a finger where it was not needed. Unlike himself, she did not mind what others said.

"Your living conditions here are a bit—" He had not meant to bring it up, but it slipped out all the same, making him feel like someone with the grease of a roast duck on his mouth commiserating with one who is starving.

"Father works at a primary school, mother works in a local factory, and what with my brother and me, none of us qualifies for an apartment. I hear that in Changzhou in Jiangsu Province they're selling houses to private buyers. I wish they were here. Still, there's so much housing going up these days that we're sure to get something sooner or later, aren't we?" She laughed again, but Song was on the verge of tears.

Here was a sorry consequence of getting new apartments: it left you with an almost unbearably more acute sense of others' hardships while at the same time your sympathy and concern lost their sincerity.

After supper, with a catch in his voice, he told his wife and son what he had decided: we ought to give Li the one-room apartment; the three-room apartment is big enough for us; even when Longlong gets married, he and his wife can have a room in this apartment.

His wife said nothing, but his son was upset. "You need suffering and adversity to live, don't you? Two days of long overdue normal life and you get uncomfortable. What a philanthropist, bestowing your little apartment on Li so that the two of you can live in poverty. What about the People's Political Consultative Conference? It claims to respect teach-

58

, and foster talent; why doesn't it concern itself with the way schoolteachers live? And all this ranting in the papers does no good, either, so what will you solve by giving Li a small apartment? Will she live there alone? Will she bring her brother? Or her parents and aunts and uncles too? How did you get the apartments anyway, theft, robbery, boot-licking, informing, or what? What do you want to let it burn a hole for?"

You scoundrel! Song cursed inwardly with a supreme attempt at self-control.

"As a matter of fact, if you were a true philanthropist and really put others before yourself and public needs before private needs, you ought to give Li both flats. You might donate your salary too."

So selfish, so plausible.

"Very well, we won't talk about it anymore. Give the apartments to whomever you like. Not that you have the right to be so generous, since you don't own them in the first place. Why hasn't auntie written lately? Do you think she could get me into an American university?"

You'd think it was raining cakes, he's so flippant, this new admirer of the West. Song lost his control. "Scoundrel!" he blurted out. Longlong's jaw dropped in a picture of innocence, and he walked out—to his own apartment.

"You shouldn't have shouted at him," said Jiang calmly. "I doubt if you know what to do yourself."

"All right, all right." Song was ashamed of his agitation. He produced a handkerchief and wiped his forehead and palms. The past was a long series of stupidity, distortion, and jumbled tracks. The future would be aging and a restful peace, a *departure* that could happen at any moment.

"It is the last opportunity to press forward. Tomorrow I am to address an audience from outside the province on my experiences, all of them approved and printed. I just

59

have to read them out. I would appear to have reached the stage of being documented and filed away. Li has a hard life."

"What I think is that you should do more real work and stop getting bogged down in meetings."

Song forced a wry, tired smile. He wanted to get up early and exercise, Taiji boxing perhaps, or crane boxing, or five birds boxing, or he could at the very least roll those Baoding Health Balls that Zhao had given him as a house-warming present and that he had never used.

Jiang put on some music, Schubert's *Trout*. In a fit of alienation from its beauty, Song thought of fish sizzling in the pan.

Next morning Song said, in a somewhat naive tone of voice, "I had a dream last night about Li giving us meat dumplings in her new home, such a nice place with lots of rooms, long corridors with parquet floors, and magnolia-shaped chandeliers. It seemed spring-like, somehow."

"That reminds me," said Jiang. "Why don't we ask Li over? I'll make her meat dumplings."

Song was in a good mood, eating Jiang's dumplings, dipped in garlic vinegar. "For my generation," he said to Li, "the pursuit of ideals and spirit is very important. Revolutionary slogans fill us with enthusiasm. We can't help it. It's the way we were brought up."

"My father has this thing about remolding his world outlook," piped up Longlong maliciously from across the table.

Li stopped eating, placed the remaining half of her dumpling in her saucer, and fixed her gaze on Longlong. "What about your good self?" she inquired with exaggerated politeness.

"Can't stand slogans. Don't believe a word of them. What I want is a motorbike, an air conditioner, and a video.

60

Then when I've got the motorbike I'll want a car. The Shanghai *Liberation Daily*'s advertising a load of Fiats for private sale. Made in Poland on an imported Italian production line."

"There you have your slogan, then: motorbike, car, air conditioner, video. None of them you have yet, therefore they are a slogan and not reality. Yet you say you can't stand slogans." She tapped her saucer unintentionally.

"What about you?" retorted Longlong with less politeness than she had used to him. "What would you prefer, a new house or a slogan?" His mouth twisted arrogantly.

"A new house, of course." Li smiled. "Haven't you read Avanti? The rich man asks him whether he wants gold or justice. Avanti says that if he were rich he would want justice, since he would have none, but as it is he is perfectly just and will take the gold." She laughed, and the others laughed with her.

"What about my father, then? What would he take?" said Longlong, unwilling to let it rest there.

"I wouldn't know," said Li, shaking her head. "He is a special top-grade teacher and my superior. These dumplings are delicious."

But Song understood what she had left unsaid. To her he was a thing of the past. Saddened, he poured a glass of port and drank to her health.

Song began to feel better after this, and came to the conclusion that he should distribute alms in the form of largesse and food. He had his social activities, and they were his duty as a responsible citizen. He spoke everywhere, wrote articles, gave press interviews, and appealed for the improved social standing and living conditions of schoolteachers, using Li as an example. An inside reference news item written by a Xinhua branch agency cited seven schoolteachers as having the worst living conditions in Dongquan. Li was one of them, and this elated Song for quite some time. Between times he talked to Jiang as they sat and drank tea and listened to music in the sitting room. They watched the opening ceremony of the Olympic Games together and saw Hou Yuzhu of the Chinese volleyball team serve the decisive ball. They entertained, too, inviting old people and young. He enjoyed talking to young people. He believed the old and the young should learn from each other instead of the old teaching and helping the young while neglecting the latter's vitality and spirit of exploration. Jiang was a wonder with dumplings and candied yams, and Song himself made passable noodles and fried fish. He lavished his foreign exchange certificates and overseas Chinese coupons on imported and good domestic wines. Life was enjoyable and kept improving. All over China, in the cities and in the countryside, houses were going up, and more and more ordinary people were moving into new apartments and leading lives that had once been the prerogative of the *bad*. Was this not a good thing? It was an excellent thing. Song began to put on weight.

Then things happened like lightning. Jiang saw the signs first and told the disbelieving Song. It was impossible. Not when the other girl's schoolmate's uncle got us the gas stove. And there's the age difference. Longlong is too practical. I'd like him better if he were more romantic.

Then one autumn night of the same year Longlong notified his parents that he had broken off with his former girlfriend and was going to marry Li.

Song and Jiang stared at each other speechlessly. Through the window he saw the leaves of a poplar tree falling silently, whitened by the light of his lamp.

It was Longlong who first brought it up. "She's four years older than I, but then Marx's wife was four years older than he."

Pragmatism. Longlong's first emulation of Marx

brought home to Song the gulf between lip service to Marxism and the genuine article.

Infuriated by his parents' silence, Longlong threw down the gauntlet. "Supposing I told you she had a baby when she went to the farm after leaving school?"

"Who?" they both exclaimed in gratifying alarm.

"You know who I mean."

"Where's the child?" they asked, again in unison.

"I didn't say there was one, did I?"

After a long silence Jiang spoke, drily. "It's your own business. We have never interfered in your business. This is a democratic family. Our only duty is to warn you to be careful. Consider the future as well as the present. And you should consider your former girlfriend too, your—moral feelings and responsibilities toward her."

"Yes, I've treated her badly."

"What didn't you like about her?" Song couldn't help asking.

"Nothing. She's been very nice to me. She's polite, she can knit and make crispy chicken. She's up to all the requirements, yours as well as mine."

"We make no requirements," protested Song. "It's your affair."

"And Li can do none of that, but she can change my life. But then, you don't understand me, so how can you understand her?" Longlong's eyes filled with tears, astonishing Song, who had never seen him like this before.

That night both Song and Jiang were worried. Song jumped out of bed to stop the clock pendulum swinging. They did not know if it would turn out well or badly, but they knew that there was nothing they could do to alter matters.

"You don't think she's—" Song wondered aloud.

"Think she's what?" asked Jiang.

"I've sunk pretty low myself, but with social morals being what they are these days—"

"Don't beat around the bush."

"I mean, could it be that she's marrying our apartments?" Song's neck was crimson with embarrassment. He had never thought that he could be so mean.

Jiang made no comment. "Longlong really loves her," she said, "and that is happiness. I'm happy too." And she broke down and sobbed, raising Song's shame and remorse to such a pitch that he felt like crawling into a hole.

They were visited by a distant uncle of Longlong's former girlfriend, a mathematics teacher, hardworking and modest, who came of his own accord when he heard of the change in his niece's love life, not to plead for her but because he and Song were old acquaintances. His niece was young and beautiful, of good family and disposition, and had no lack of suitors. He could not, though, understand Longlong, whom he would have congratulated if he had found another girl quite so angelically pretty. But this? What was the matter with the lad? Should he see a psychiatrist? It was a classic case of letting it burn a hole in your pocket.

Song said nothing.

Jiang nodded. "Yes, it is a shame, and we've let her down. We'd do our best to talk to him again, but to tell you the truth he was quite adamant. From what I could see it would be difficult to make him change his mind. Ah well!"

She related the conversation to Longlong, not omitting the bit about holes in pockets. He bowed his head, and Song noticed two *gray hairs* on the head of his twenty-six-year-old, unmarried son, in a lock that drooped sadly. Oh, the *shock*! His only son, so often the butt of his disapproval, was getting gray hairs. *Young people* must be going gray *earlier* than their parents had, then, perhaps because their parents had believed in slogans and they didn't. Or could it be that what their parents saw as flippancy was another form of agony that also wasted youth, life, and soul?

"Holes in pockets, yes." Longlong looked up with burning eyes. "I see it more and more clearly. There is a kind of *hole in the pocket* that belongs to *human nature*, that shows it isn't time for your memorial service yet." He lowered his voice and went on. "And there's more of it still, I'm afraid, because Li and I are accepting teaching jobs in Qinghai. To be exact, in the Yushu Autonomous Zhou. They have offered us a raise in salary plus a lot of subsidies. They'll give us housing. But we'll have more than housing."

Jaws dropped.

"Supposing your aunt writes?"

"Fine. I hope to go to the United States in three years, preferably with Li. We've signed a three-year contract with the Autonomous Zhou."

"You want to go to Qinghai *and* America?"

"It's about as farfetched as mixing fire and water, isn't it, if you listen to the top filmmakers, not to mention special top-grade teachers? And when we've done that, we wouldn't mind Antarctica."

He might have been talking in a dream, and it was nonetheless affecting for that. Return the right of dreaming to the young. The wind on the Qinghai plateau is real. Song and Jiang, who knew how strong that wind could be, felt a warmth, a thaw in their hardened hearts.

An earthquake shook the foundations of his hard-won house.

Very good. You are like us when we were young.

Yes, and we no longer are. That was the truth. An uncontrollable sadness gripped Song's heart, and he kissed his son, feeling, guiltily, how slim the lad was while he put on weight day by day. He had intermittent spells of dizziness these days with ringing in the ears, which the gastrodia pills and the ginseng royal jelly did little to alleviate. A doctor said he had Ménière's syndrome. A brain surgeon wanted to check him for a tumor. An orthopedist wanted to X-ray the vertebrae in his neck. Yet he could still suffer. He could still feel the torment of his soul and the burning anxiety that came with life. He had never thought that dying would bring him contentment. He was still burning holes. He could still do foolish things.

He could still feel the wind of the plateau blowing wildly in his heart, the wind that was beckoning to his son and his daughter-in-law.

A Winter's Topic

In City V, capital of N Province, there lived a "young" old man who was locally and internationally famous. At sixty-three and not quite 1.62 meters tall, Zhu Shendu had white hair, ruddy cheeks, and hearty spirits. He was head of a branch of Academia Sinica, president of the science association, and because he had written a few short stories in his youth, also president of the Federation of Writers and Artists and president of the local branch of the Chinese Writers' Association. He was one of the leaders of a democratic party branch in City V, most of the members of which were intellectuals; he joined the Communist Party in 1981, and when his probationary period ended in 1982, became a full member.

He was a physiologist by profession, though his fame came not from new contributions to the field of anatomy or bodily functions, or, of course, decidedly not from those mawkish (his own term) writings of his youth. He was famous primarily because he was one of the world's rare authorities on balneology.

Balneation is simply bathing, and there is nothing strange about that. But there aren't very many people who can give a scientific explanation or summary of the subject. N Province had never been big on bathing: following age-old tradition, a person bathed only two or three times in a lifetime. Most people bathed twice, once at birth and once at death. Confucians, bureaucrats, and the rich bathed three times, the extra bath at marriage.

Zhu Shendu's grandfather, influenced by Western thought in the late nineteenth century, waged a bold and ruthless attack on the traditions of his forefathers by building a bathhouse, advocating bathing and even brazenly suggesting that everyone could bathe once a month, which, for the time, was an act of earth-shattering heresy. Later, charged with the crimes of fallacy and corruption, he died in prison. Five years after his death the emperor of the Qing Dynasty redressed his case and dubbed him posthumously an "upright gentleman of the Qing."

Henceforth, bathing in N Province gradually caught on. Someone doing textual research on *The Great Learning*[1] found a commentary suggesting that fasting in addition to bathing promoted sincerity and thought, rectification of the mind, cultivation of the person, regulation of the family, good government of the state, and peace throughout the kingdom. Thus bathing gained documentation and correct interpretation, and the gentry came to consider it a worthy tradition. The following generation, Zhu Shendu's father, Zhu Yixin, provoked outcry anew, however, by building a bathhouse open to women. Upright gentlemen suggested that Zhu Yixin was turning virtuous women into prostitutes by opening what was in fact a brothel. The substance of the dispute entirely overran the bounds of bathing. For a time the gentry in N Province considered Zhu Yixin a scourge, and the cry "The licentiousness won't stop until Yixin is dead" resounded far and wide. It was said that a virtuous woman had been so enraged by the sordid suggestion that

1. A Confucian classic.

she visit Zhu Yixin's bathhouse that she grabbed scissors and cut off her left earlobe, which had heard the "devilish seduction." This "model of female virtue" was entered in the V County annals. (V did not become a city until thirty years ago.)

From boyhood, Zhu Shendu carried on the rebellious, nonconformist, progressive, trailblazing, dare-to-be-first spirit of his forefathers. While conducting physiological research and writing "mawkish" prose on the side, he was determined to establish the new field of bathing. He spent fifteen years writing the seven-volume *Introduction to Bathing*, which contained chapters on "Bathing and the Body," "Bathing and the Circulatory System," "Bathing and the Digestive System," "Bathing and the Respiratory System," "Bathing and the Skin," "Bathing and the Hair," "Bathing and the Skeleton," "Bathing and Mental Hygiene," "Bathing and Puberty," "Bathing and the Hygiene of Menopause," "Bathing and the Family," "Bathing and the Nation," "Bathing for Workers and Miners," "Bathing in Wartime," "Bathing and Water," "Bathing and Soap," "Bathtubology," "Bathrobeology," "The Science of Back Scrubbing," "The Science of Massage," "Bathing Methodology," "Studies on Water Temperature," "Bath-towelology," "Side Effects of Bathing," "Bathing and Politics," "Historical Perspectives on Bathing," "Bathing and Antibathing," "To Bathe or Not to Bathe," "Bathing Limits," "Tests of Bathing Results," "Unexpurgated Studies on Bathing," and "Further Unexpurgated Studies on Bathing, I to VII"—all in all an imposing tome at the forefront of the modern world.

Introduction to Bathing was translated into a dozen foreign languages, and two constitutional monarchies awarded Zhu Shendu honorary degrees on the basis of his seven-volume magnum opus. It seemed that for the past five thousand years and five hundred years to come, in China and abroad, Zhu Shendu was firmly ensconced on the throne of bathing studies.

Flocks of visitors entered and left Zhu Shendu's living room nightly, particularly a group of young worshipers. The youngsters chirped and twittered, laughed merrily and talked endlessly, unable to tear themselves away from the Venerable Zhu's seven-volume work. Some had the uncanny ability to recite passages word for word. Others were such good talkers that on first hearing it seemed they had strayed far from the subject to somewhere off in the clouds, or between heaven and the deep blue sea, but they were always able to end up with a certain phrase (including punctuation) from a certain line on a certain page of a certain volume of the seven-volume opus, thus winning Zhu's good graces as well. Some stuttered and stammered but expressed a kind of pious devotion or blind loyalty to Zhu all the same. Some were so eloquent they were almost unctuous, but they never went too far. The group revolved around him like the planets around the sun, gathered at his feet like a flock around their shepherd, and a good time was had by all.

Outstanding among them was a willowy lass who looked both older and younger than she was, spoke in a childish voice, kept taking off and putting on her glasses, and appeared quite fetching when she pouted. Naturally, she was the leader of the young group. Her name was Yu Qiuping.

Life in V grew better all the time, and life for Zhu Shendu grew better, if more regimented, as well. A new hardcover edition of his seven-volume opus was about to come out, and he spent four months meticulously going over the original, changing in all seven words and six punctuation marks. He also made new suggestions for the layout and typeface and asked Yu Qiuping to draft for him an afterword of 752 words for the new edition. He was rather enjoying it all. Yu Qiuping announced that when she finished the afterword, she intended to work on *Zhu Shendu: A Critical Biography* and asked him to arrange a chronology of photos of himself from boyhood to the present and to pull together his handwritten manuscripts. Venerable Zhu smiled with pleasure but said, "Oh, go on! Why bother?"

If it hadn't been for the Zhao Xiaoqiang incident, Zhu Shendu's fine days would have continued to tick by as regularly and predictably as European clockwork.

At eight P.M. on November 22, 1983, Yu Qiuping flew into Dr. Zhu Shendu's living room, flushed with agitation and popping a shiny blue button from her coat as she removed it. Her greeting, lacking its usual sweet lilt, sounded rushed and irritated. Zhu Shendu furrowed his brow, and raised his eyelids, only to find Yu Qiuping blurting out before she'd even taken a seat, "Zhao's come out and publicly contradicted you!"

"Which Zhao? What do you mean, contradicted?" Zhu Shendu had no idea what she was talking about.

"That Zhao Xiaoqiang!"

"Which Zhao Xiaoqiang?" Zhu Shendu, with great displeasure, squeezed the syllables Zhao Xiaoqiang through his teeth as if discussing a microbe with a strange name in a stool sample.

"I mean that bastard," said Yu Qiuping, her words slurred with impatience. "His mother's divorced. When he was in primary school, he stole pears from the trees in the park. . . . You know, he went to Canada and stayed there three years raising goldfish. He's published an article saying bath time should be in the morning!"

Zhu Shendu had just caught a buzzing past his ears. "What? In the morning?" He stammered, "If you can ba-ba-bathe in the morn-morn-morn-morning, then you can talk with your he-he-heel and a roo-roo-roo-rooster can lay eggs!"

Yu Qiuping opened her imitation-leather handbag and pulled out the local evening paper, page three of which carried Zhao Xiaoqiang's signed column, "Canadian Tidbits." Then it took her a while to find Dr. Zhu's reading glasses. He finally put them on and found the crucial phrase, which Yu Qiuping had underlined in red.

"Here in China most people bathe before going to bed at night, but in Canada people *prefer* [emphasis added by Yu Qiuping] to bathe first thing in the morning. . . ."

Look as he might over page three of the paper, there was only this one sentence, albeit underlined in red; right next to it was "General Knowledge for Everyday Life: How to Eliminate Bad Breath." It evoked only a "hmph" from Dr. Zhu.

"To tell the truth," said Yu Qiuping, pursing her cute little mouth, the lower lip of which was moving in and out like a tiny shovel, "bathing in the morning versus bathing at night is no small matter. What's so great about Zhao Xiaoqiang? Isn't it just that he's been to Canada? Is the moon in Canada any rounder than ours? Offer me a chance to go to Canada and I wouldn't even take it! What makes him think he's so great just because he's been to Canada? What makes him so sure Canadian bathing practices are correct? Are the people here in City V Canadians? Have the workers, cadres, and peasants, who make up 90-some percent of the population of our city, ever been to Canada? If Canadians don't respect their elders then and we shouldn't either? Besides, Canada is. . . ."

His head about to burst with an earful of nothing but Canada, Zhu Shendu waved his hand and said, "He's just a child, pay him no mind."

At this point the doorbell rang. His other three favorite students had come to seethe over the "preposterous argument" of the conceited Zhao Xiaoqiang. They stressed how disrespectful Zhao Xiaoqiang was being toward Venerable Zhu and added that if he kept it up, the whole field of bathing studies would be undermined at its foundations.

"Oh, do be quiet," Venerable Zhu snapped. "A milksop still wet behind the ears who goes abroad for a look around and picks up what people are saying, then jacks his own jaws about it, isn't even worth the time of day!" Having finished, he gave a big yawn, and the sharp aspiration set his vocal cords aquiver with a sound like the cock-a-doodle-doo of a rooster. This was his customary signal for guests to leave, but tonight it seemed to have an added note of gloom for some reason.

Zhu Shendu had actually been quite magnanimous that night, but two days later it was all over town that "Zhu Shendu's mad," "Zhu Shendu said Zhao Xiaoqiang is to big for his britches," "Venerable Zhu called Zhao Xiaoqiang a goddamned bastard," "Professor Zhu said Zhao Xiaoqiang's a no-good," "Dr. Zhu said Zhao Xiaoqiang farts foreign," "Zhu Shendu said. . . ."

The news ran without legs to stand on, and every last bit of it reached Zhao Xiaoqiang.

Zhao Xiaoqiang also had a bunch of buddies who revolved around him. The most dynamic among them was a lame and lanky youth who had grown a beard when still young and whose big eyes resembled a woman's. His name was Li Lili. He slapped his palm angrily and said, "They're uncultured and uneducated; they're bullheaded and ignorant and can't do anything. That bath study of theirs is all bullshit! There's only one mission fit for them—destination: crematorium!"

Zhao Xiaoqiang was a biologist and often used goldfish for experiments on genetic variations, hence Yu Qiuping's insult about his spending three years in Canada raising goldfish. He never anticipated that his article on the back page of the evening paper would cause such a fuss, and he rather regretted having written such nonsense. He sternly put a stop to Li Lili's attack on Zhu Shendu, saying, "Professor Zhu has his accomplishments. His family has advocated bathing for generations, which has done wonders for progress here in City V. His historic contributions are beyond doubt. His Japanese is not bad either. Venerable Zhu has always supported and been good to me. Without Professor Zhu's recommendation, I couldn't have gone to study in Canada. He's my mentor, and as my conscience is my guide, I've never dared forget it. This is all the result of a few little misunderstandings, and once they're cleared up, everything will be fine."

Li Lili's lips trembled with rage as he pointed at Zhao Xiaoqiang and said, "Bookworm! Egghead! The more you study, the less sinks in! In Lin Biao's famous words, when heads start to roll, you won't even know why."

Zhao Xiaoqiang just laughed. He'd always welcomed visitors like Li Lili. They'd talk and laugh together, and sometimes he even got something out of it, but he wasn't like them. He neither could nor would gather them around him and become their "spiritual leader." He had no need to let and had never considered letting Li Lili and his lot become his cabinet, his assistants, his think tank, or his palanquin bearers. When they spoke, when they offered information, he just listened. He had his own life, his own opinions, and his own way of thinking.

The next day he tried to call Zhu Shendu on the phone, but couldn't get through in the morning. He finally got through at noon, but Zhu Shendu was in the middle of lunch, and when he heard that Zhao Xiaoqiang was on the line, he wouldn't take the call. When Zhao called again twenty-two minutes later, he was told that Venerable Zhu was already napping. Whenever he tried again later in the afternoon, the line was always busy. At five o'clock he thought to hell with it and went to see him. Zhu Shendu treated him coldly. Their talk of the weather was stiff and somewhat stilted. The conversation inevitably came around to Canada. Zhu Shendu said, "It's no good looking down on everything just because you've been to Canada." Zhao Xiaoqiang readily agreed, but felt it wasn't enough. He stammered, "In that article I wrote for the paper I just happened to mention bathing. I certainly wasn't out to get anybody . . ."

Before he could finish, Zhu Shendu leapt out of his chair with a shout. He really was a spry old thing. He said, "Please do not discuss it with me. I never asked you here for a lecture on bathing. Am I not uncultured? Uneducated? Am I not bullheaded and ignorant and can't do anything? Isn't there only one mission fit for me—destination: crematorium?"

Zhao Xiaoqiang was dumbfounded. How could what Li Lili had said in his home less than twenty-four hours earlier have reached Zhu Shendu's ears so quickly, virtually word for word? Could Zhu have bugged his house? It would be better if he had, for then he'd know that that nonsense hadn't come from Zhao Xiaoqiang, that he hadn't even agreed to it. On the contrary, he had sternly put a stop to it. Of course, he still couldn't shirk the blame, because those things had been said in his house, because he had provided Li Lili with the time and space in which to say them, because he had entertained the person who had uttered those irresponsible, yes, abusive words. The logic was quite simple: Li Lili had not said those things in Zhu Shendu's home, nor had he delivered them in a speech at a major intersection. No, he had spouted that nonsense right in his home. Could he say it had nothing to do with him? Could he explain everything to Zhu Shendu, clear himself, ditch Li Lili, then join Zhu Shendu in lambasting him?

He fumbled for words, started to say something, but stopped. When Zhu Shendu had first heard those things, he hadn't really believed them, but as soon as he got angry, he mentioned them all. His anger was real, but whether those things were true or not, he still couldn't be sure. The way Zhao Xiaoqiang was acting convinced him he had really said those things. Otherwise, why hadn't he flatly denied it? Good little Zhao Xiaoqiang had actually called him those vicious names! When he thought of this, he nearly fainted with rage.

Zhao Xiaoqiang trudged home with a heavy heart, Zhu Shendu's angry shouts ringing in his ears, and the image of Zhu Shendu boiling with rage dancing before his eyes, especially the way he inhaled sharply and pressed his lips so tight together that the upper lip had nearly vanished, as straight as if it had been cut by a knife, an expression that Zhao Xiaoqiang found particularly upsetting. He truly regretted having so blithely gone to see Venerable Zhu—he had just been asking for it. Walking along with his mind elsewhere, he was nearly hit by a Toyota Crown as he crossed an intersection. Three cars, all coming from and heading in different directions, screeched to a halt in front of him. The traffic cop and the drivers of the cars all yelled at him. Then he was taken aside by the cop for another lecture. Without hearing a single word the cop was saying, he just kept nodding his head in agreement to the rhythm of that monotonous jumble of sound. "Your attitude's not bad; I won't fine you this time. But next time watch where you're going!" When he finally realized that the cop's last instruction was letting him off, he smiled.

He stayed on the corner for a couple of minutes look-

ing at a giant movie poster under the lights—*Our Niu Baisui.*
A fat peasant seated on a *kang*[2] was holding chopsticks and
bowl and turning slightly, most likely to coax his angry wife
to eat. Zhao Xiaoqiang thought life was really funny, and tiring. But his spirits had brightened somewhat.

When he got home, he and his wife ate dinner watching the evening news on TV, which showed several scenes of
state leaders receiving foreign guests. The guests were all
poised and frank, and even the carpets, armchairs, tea sets,
chandeliers, and paintings on the walls gave off a certain ex-
pansiveness. Zhao Xiaoqiang felt greatly inspired. The next
program was *One World,* which was introducing an African
country that night, moving from busy, modern cities to desert as far as the eye could see, to primitive dancing. Then an
entertainment hour came on with flashing colored lights and
strutting singing stars—it was enough to make one laugh.

The next morning, when Zhao Xiaoqiang's co-
workers brought up the bathing dispute with him, he gave a
leisurely smile nearly fit for receiving foreign guests and
said, "Actually, it's good to discuss these issues, to let all
voices be heard on the bathing subject. What's so terrible
about each airing his view, a lively debate?" He continued,
"Of course, I have complete respect for Zhu Shendu, and I
fully recognize his achievements in the field of bath studies,
but that is not to say that his every word on the subject is the
ultimate truth, and it doesn't mean that I can't give an objec-
tive report on some conditions in Canada or offer a few different, supplementary, or debatable views!"

Zhao Xiaoqiang discovered that though he had spoken quite sincerely, naturally, and calmly, most of his listeners seemed puzzled, confused, and even uneasy.

Zhu Shendu felt somewhat chagrined at having lost

2. A heatable brick bed.

control that night with Zhao Xiaoqiang, but he was the kind of person who, the more he found himself in the wrong, the more he took it out on someone else. He firmly believed that if it weren't for the hostility, provocation, or enticement of others, or the damage they caused, he would never do anything wrong himself. Naturally he couldn't lower himself to the level of that infant, so, a few days later, he let a few magnanimous words drop in certain settings. "Fine. Bring on the debate! How to make bathing more sensible is always open to discussion! . . . My book is certainly not the last word on the subject; the truth isn't just what one person says. Young people disdain authority; there's nothing wrong with daring to raise new questions, new views! We've disdained authority for generations! We're all old hands at bucking tradition, going against the grain! I come from a long line of tradition buckers!" He added things like, "The more truth is debated, the clearer it becomes. True gold does not fear the test of fire. Truth emerges in triumph over falsehood." These statements made him the spokesman for truth and made what he said sound grand and heroic.

The words of each reached the ears of the other. At the time, news was even coming out of Political Bureau meetings, not to mention other places! When they'd both heard what the other had said, naturally a truce followed, and everything calmed down somewhat.

But the bathing dispute had already become an early winter topic of conversation both inside and outside intellectual circles in City V and even a considerable portion of N Province. Along with criticism of Zhang Xiaotian's novel *The Luxuriant Grassland,* the down jackets on sale in City V, and the story of a spoiled girl who had killed her mother with rat poison because she hadn't bought her a Popsicle and then was strangled by her father, who, after killing his six-year-old, hanged himself, the bath dispute between the old and the young had drawn the attention of people from all walks of life in the city. The questions on everyone's lips were: How did their "relationship trouble" happen? What was the background to the fight? They thirsted to discover the deep mysteries of the matter.

Different people went to the two of them separately to ask these questions. Zhao Xiaoqiang reluctantly told them of his article on the back page of the evening paper. Zhu Shendu equally reluctantly mentioned the morning-versus-evening bathing issue. These answers invariably disappointed those who heard them; everyone felt this difference of opinion was not terribly significant, nor was it terribly interesting, and it certainly was not sufficient grounds for such dramatic tension in their relationship. Zhu Shendu and Zhao Xiaoqiang each denied having "relationship trouble" with the other, but this highly secretive behavior seemed only to corroborate its severity and depth. "Differences," "hidden facts," or "both problems in the past and a real clash now" were what most people thought.

It seemed some people in City V in N Province had made a hobby of analyzing other people's "relationship trouble." Moreover, they seemed to have the methods and efficacy of an amateur F.B.I or National Security Council. It wasn't long before they had dug up stacks of background material and produced a considerable amount of classified information. Yu Qiuping and her friends discovered that Zhao Xiaoqiang was dissatisfied with his work unit, job, salary, and living conditions. When he returned from his gilding abroad, Zhao Xiaoqiang had been intent on being named head of the Biological Research Institute of Academia Sinica and had hoped for a promotion of two grades and a raise of three on the pay scale, a three-room apartment, nomination as a research fellow, and entrance into a good high school for his only daughter, who had just started middle school. None of these things had come to pass, so, wondering whether the old authority Zhu Shendu had blocked him, he had become resentful and suspicious and had waited for his chance to attack Zhu's prestige as a way to vent his anger. Someone else came up with additional information to the effect that once, at a scientists' social gathering, Zhao Xiaoqiang had offered his hand to Zhu Shendu, but Zhu Shendu, because he had been wrapped up in conversation with the local political consultative conference chairman, had failed to notice Zhao's awkwardly outstretched hand, and the unintentional slight had greatly wounded Zhao Xiaoqiang's pride.

Li Lili and his friends concentrated their efforts on analyzing the fact that whoever wanted to get in with academic or artistic circles in City V spent all his time running over to Zhu Shendu's, where, once in the door, his worth grew tenfold. Whoever joined the Zhu family got what amounted to a special license to do business, a green light at every corner. But Zhao Xiaoqiang was upright by nature and quite bookish, and it had been a whole month after his return from Canada before he had visited Zhu. Zhu had borne a grudge and considered him an eyesore ever since. Someone added in hushed tones the "top secret" that an agronomist in City V called Professor Shi Kanlü was Zhu Shendu's longtime rival and that the day after Zhao Xiaoqiang returned from Canada he had paid a call on Professor Shi and given him two jars of instant coffee, one of Coffeemate, an electric razor, a clock radio with six functions, and two large packages of Western health tonic. But it had been a month and a half before he'd gone to see Zhu Shendu, and he brought him only one carton of 555 cigarettes and a Camel-brand lighter. This unequal treatment had sown the seeds of discontent.

Thus the matter moved from historical observations to the psychological to a deeper level of character analysis. Some said that the older Zhu Shendu got, the more he was prone to jealously; he wouldn't let anybody better him at anything. "Zhu Shendu's a jealous old man," they'd say, laughing. Some depicted Zhao Xiaoqiang as young and aggressive, sitting on top of the world looking down on everyone, determined to let no one stand in his way. Moving on to political and journalistic observations, everyone tossed around phrases like "junior faction versus senior faction," "new party versus old party," and "foreign versus local" adeptly and with great relish.

In short, nearly every amateur relationship research analyst agreed that the "Zhu-Zhao conflict" was by no means fortuitous, that it was part of a pattern and unavoidable, and that there was more to it than met the eye. In short, it was a concrete instance in City V of the deep social and generational conflicts found virtually everywhere.

There were quite a few people, many of them young, who were delighted, invigorated, positively set drooling to catch wind of a conflict. A group of them would get together over firewater, fried shrimp chips, and fossilized eggs to probe the significance, secret findings, latest trends, future predictions—the whole story of the fight between Zhu and Zhao. They could go from morning to night, from early evening to midnight without a break. They could cite the same material thirty-three times in a single conversation. On the question of Zhao Xiaoqiang's presents to Professor Shi, for example, every account provided minor embellishments with slight variations. No one grew tired; the thirty-third hearing remained as fresh as the first; the thirty-third rendition came complete with all the dancing eyes, dramatic face, slapping of the palm, and stamping of the feet—all the earnest display of the first time some secret finding was disclosed. Fascination with human conflict is truly boundless! The Spring and Autumn and Warring States periods' tradition of choosing sides has lasted through the ages and is with us to this day. Nothing can match it! A weakness for relation-shipology is enough to foster group after group of relationship fanatics. China's "contact explosion" and "name list explosion" are enough to rival the "sexual explosion" and "information explosion" of the West. Chinese fiction writers treat love, life, and death, the unknown, philosophy, and human nature; they write scenes of everyday life, detective stories, scar literature[3], stream of consciousness; they write of the beauty of human nature, and they create stock characters, but they'd be better off writing about human relationships, about power struggles between people, which, in most cases, are power struggles between good people! For only then could they strike a nerve deep in the reader's soul that is imbued with a sense of history, homeland, the collective unconscious, the past and the present! Only then could they appeal to both refined and popular tastes, produce works both timely and timeless, for young and old alike, required reading both at home and on the road!

With analysis of the situation complete, people sprang into action. They went off to see Zhu Shendu or Zhao Xiaoqiang or, one rank down, Yu Qiuping or Li Lili to "take sides." "Take sides" is one of the many terms coined during the "cultural revolution"; it means to stand with a certain person (or, in the expression of the time, to take a certain line). "Taking sides" is like shooting craps or betting on a certain horse at the races in old Shanghai or present-day Hong Kong. Some people believe it is a short-cut to victory on the battlefield of life. So some sought out Zhao Xiaoqiang and started right in lambasting Zhu Shendu. The lambasting was so extensive that Zhao Xiaoqiang couldn't even follow it. Others sought out Zhu Shendu and used Zhao Xiaoqiang to expound upon the evils of society, academics, and youth

3. Writings on "cultural revolution" (1966–76) sufferings.

82

today. Some visited Yu Qiuping with reports of Zhao Xiaoqiang's childhood misdeeds; the tale of how his daughter had scratched a classmate's face in kindergarten was mentioned on the logical grounds of "like father, like daughter; like daughter, like father." A tale that Li Lili had heard and passed on about how Zhu Shendu's wife had mistreated their amah began to crop up in certain circles. Things got to the point where even someone who had studied under one of Zhao Xiaoqiang's teachers years before him, a man who had made something of a name for himself in City V, was thirteen years older, and earned a salary six pay grades higher than Zhao Xiaoqiang, found a chance to take his hand, look him straight in the eye, and say, his breath hot on Zhao Xiaoqiang's face, "There's plenty of time, Comrade Xiaoqiang; you just wait. You'll see that I'm behind you all the way!" Zhao Xiaoqiang felt sick and very nearly lost his dinner of the night before—two bowls of pork and chives wonton soup.

A long-haired youth who was skilled in power *qigong*[4] and had published two short stories in the evening paper came up to Zhu Shendu and said, "I saw through that damned Zhao Xiaoqiang a long time ago! Sir, you just think well of me, and when the time is ripe, just give me a nod and I'll be at your service."

After that, for some reason, Zhu Shendu's heart rate remained accelerated for a full twenty-four hours. He was seriously afraid that that long-haired lad would use power *qigong* or some telekinetic power to take Zhao Xiaoqiang's young life.

Those who were sharper that most didn't "take sides" at all. They greeted Venerable Zhu with a broad smile and Young Zhao smiling broadly. They greeted Young Zhao

4. A form of martial arts.

with the usual pleasantries and Venerable Zhu with pleasantries as usual. They were cordial and light with Venerable Zhu and light and cordial with Young Zhao. For them it was six of one, half a dozen of the other, with not a nickel's worth of difference between the two of them. They were very careful not to lean an inch toward either side.

Both Venerable Zhu and Young Zhao found the whole thing terribly boring and perverse, but they couldn't escape or protest. Venerable Zhu couldn't very well turn on or shoo off Yu Qiuping, could he? Young Zhao couldn't very well do the same to Li Lili, could he? They couldn't very well pull the rug out from under their own feet and leave themselves isolated. Young Zhao bolstered himself with the thought that there was nothing new under the sun and he could just ignore it all. Venerable Zhu comforted himself with the notions that a great man holds no grudge against the wrongs of a lesser man, a doctor's mind is impartial, a learned man is not impulsive. But both had sunk into the mire of being sympathized with, told secrets, and given advice; they had been cast as factional leaders and could not extricate themselves from the roles.

Gradually, the topic began to grow somewhat stale, and those who had been so devoted to it turned instead to analyzing who would be the new mayor of City V.

A little magazine published in Beijing printed in its January 1984 issue a report entitled "A Student Back from Abroad on Contention," written by a staff reporter, one of Zhao Xiaoqiang's old classmates, who had interviewed him over six months earlier. Zhao Xiaoqiang had long since forgotten all about it and remembered only when he received two copies of the issue.

The article "basically" stuck to the truth but was spiced up in no small measure with inflammatory detail. Zhao Xiaoqiang's mind was put to rest, however, when he reminded himself that a reporter's talent was demonstrated by precisely this kind of inflammatory writing, that certain reporters and writers of reportage depended on nothing if not inflammatory writing to win names for themselves and the appreciation of the reading public.

"On Contention" quoted Zhao Xiaoqiang as saying, "We sorely lack contention, discussion of things and events rather than people, the 'I-love-my-teacher-but-I-love-truth-more' spirit! When I was abroad, I often encountered people having heated arguments over certain issues during scholarly debates, but afterward they were still the best of friends. Here in China we've been talking about contention for decades and it's never even gotten off the ground. Why? Because right from the start you can't get past the barrier of offending people. If you venture to offer a different view, people think you're out to get someone, that you're attacking someone, that you're challenging or provoking someone, and right there you'll have offended one, ten, a hundred, thousands! In the end, you've actually even *forgotten* what you were contending and why. All you remember is that the two sides have sworn to fight to the death, and it never stops, a hopeless mess! If things go on like this, how can scholarship possibly prosper?"

Zhao Xiaoqiang was further quoted as saying, "It's easy to say everyone is equal before the truth, but how hard it is to practice! Age and seniority, not to mention power, influence, authority, position, and one's immediate supervisor are always the real criteria for truth! When debating with the old and venerable, it doesn't matter who is right and who is wrong, because the question of one's attitude comes first. Presumptuous and arrogant—those two words can settle any scholarly debate!"

The article ended with a flowery description of Zhao Xiaoqiang. "He crossed the mighty Pacific to seek learning in another land. Handsome and dedicated, he discussed his ambitions openly and cheerfully. His profound and incisive comments are punctuated with dramatic gestures. He is a breath of fresh air for the academic circles of this homeland; he is a harbinger of spring!"

Damn!

Zhao Xiaoqiang groaned and sighed and couldn't sit still. His wife spent hours trying to console him. "It's perfectly clear, since that interview took place over six months ago, that you couldn't have been out to get anyone. And if they don't believe it, they can write to Beijing and ask. Anyway, you didn't write that article; it was that old classmate of yours who came here drinking Canadian whisky who wrote that spiced-up flowery stuff."

"And what good will it do to say that? Who's going to look into it for you? When Wu Han wrote *Hai Rui Dismissed from Office,* the Lushan meeting hadn't even been held, yet everyone insisted it was written to protest Peng Dehuai's dismissal.[5] Who is going to listen to reason?"

"Things are different now!"

"I never said they weren't!"

Meanwhile, the article exploded like an atom bomb before Zhu Shendu's eyes. Yu Qiuping didn't stammer nervously this time, and she hadn't even underlined anything in red; she just fluttered up to Venerable Zhu and handed him the magazine and his bifocals.

Venerable Zhu took a full forty-five minutes to read the short article, savoring every word, every sentence. First his face reddened, then turned green, then yellow, then white; the more he read, the more clearheaded he grew, until finally calm transcended anger and humiliation condensed

5. Peng Dehuai was dismissed at the Lushan meeting of the Party Central Committee.

86

into indifference. He finished the article without a sound, just smiling weakly, his upper lip pulled ever so slightly inward.

Yu Qiuping acted with unusual perspicacity this time. Eyeing Venerable Zhu's expression with satisfaction, she slipped out without a word.

Zhu Shendu lay awake all night with crackling ears and burning mouth. That Zhao Xiaoqiang was attacking from all fronts and landing countless blows!

Morning, evening—who cares! We can't play up to Canada and slight China. How could we face our ancestors? How could we face this great land of ours? How could we face our revolutionary martyrs, our teachers? Thinking these things, Zhu Shendu felt his blood boil and hot tears well up in his eyes. He'd stake his life on it; he couldn't let Zhao Xiaoqiang's heresy reign! Death would be no great loss. A little integrity, hands clean, a bag of bones—what was it worth? The seven-volume *Introduction to Bathing*—not a tear. Three generations with the determination to move mountains, and everlasting achievements—all laughed away! But we can't endure rebellion and disgrace! A scholar can suffer death but not humiliation! If I hear the truth in the morning, I can die content in the evening! A poor scholar lives for fame and integrity! If traitors like Zhao Xiaoqiang can prevail, China will no longer be China, bathing no longer bathing, and I'll not rest in my grave!

A sense of sublime sorrow left Zhu Shendu feeling righteous and noble.

Starting the next day, Zhu Shendu shuttled in and out of party, government, mass organization, military, industrial, agricultural, and commercial offices and talked about the Zhao Xiaoqiang affair in every department and work unit. He spoke seriously, earnestly, and appropriately, without personal attack, irritation, or any emotion whatsoever. On the contrary, he stressed that he was discussing "things and events, not people." He spoke of Zhao Xiaoqiang's youth, talent, and promise, and emphasized that it was precisely because he held such high hopes for him that he suffered such extraordinary grief and sadness over his mistake. He went on to say that he was about to give up all his public posts in order to devote himself to scholarship, and that there was no reason why bathing issues could not continue to be discussed in a calm and deliberate manner. He welcomed comments and criticism on *Introduction to Bathing;* his mottoes had always been "Pride goeth before a fall" and "Be happy to stand corrected." He could not, however, remain silent on a matter of such great significance, and he could not refrain from stating his position clearly, for to do otherwise would be to sin against his country, his people, and science!

After several such addresses he still wasn't sure he had convinced his listeners, but he had certainly convinced himself. He was so conscientious! He was too sincere! He was too earnest! Too revolutionary! He had bravely come forward! He had pledged his life to the defense! He hadn't been moved by such righteous indignation in a long, long time. "In the gathering dusk stands a sturdy pine, tranquil as tumultuous clouds sweep past." "Only from the raging seas can true heroism arise."[6] No doubt about it, this was a debate on major issues of principle, a question of which flag to wave, which road to take, which steps to take!

What is truly within will be manifested without, and his fervent indignation brought him back to the brink of tears! The solemn and stirring mood quickly infected Yu Qiuping and her friends, and impassioned talk was heard all over town.

It moved the editor-in-chief and other editors of the city's evening paper, the editor responsible for publishing

6. Lines from Mao Zedong's poems.

"Canadian Tidbits" most deeply of all. In trepidation and great anguish he was determined to make up for his error. Articles vaguely critical of Zhao Xiaoqiang began to appear in the paper. One was commentary on "thinking the moon in Canada is rounder that the moon in China." Another discussed how "some people who occupy landlords' manors have taken up the opium pipes and concubines of the landlords." All were impressively written.

Things in this world are interesting indeed. With Zhu Shendu's impassioned presentations and the paper's discourse on the moon, opium pipes, and concubines, Zhao Xiaoqiang's image suddenly grew suspect. All kinds of rumors flowed in City V and within a circumference of four hundred kilometers around it. "Zhao Xiaoqiang favors getting rid of chopsticks and switching to knives and forks. Zhao Xiaoqiang advocates closing all bathhouses at seven A.M. Zhao Xiaoqiang put green eyeliner on his wife. Zhao Xiaoqiang supports abolishing the Chinese language and adopting Canadian instead." These rumors developed into: "Zhao Xiaoqiang has a girlfriend in Canada and he's prepared to divorce his wife and emigrate to Canada; he's already applied for citizenship. Zhao Xiaoqiang's girlfriend wrote him a letter calling him 'Dear.' Customs is holding forty Walkmans Zhao Xiaoqiang brought back from abroad. Zhao Xiaoqiang brought pornography back with him. Zhao Xiaoqiang was searched at customs and found carrying a new kind of American contraceptive!"

Some of the Zhaos' enthusiastic friends made special trips to see them; others promptly reported whenever they ran into them, some sent registered or regular letters, and others phoned, so that not a day went by that the Zhaos were not informed as to the latest developments in the rumors. Some reports were delivered with such diligence, detail, frequency, excitement, and well-focused powers of observation that Zhao and his wife seriously considered whether perhaps these rumors had been manufactured and spread by the very people who were pledging such loyalty and reporting them. They soon decided against that, however, for on those grounds they'd have no way of telling the good from the bad and everyone would be suspect, which would just be self-defeating, serving only to isolate themselves from everyone.

An hour later Zhao Xiaoqiang said to his wife, "What a mess! I think our paranoia just now was a bit sick. In Canada people in such a state would see a psychiatrist for analysis. In some cases medication is required. I heard that the mental hospital here in the city started offering counseling, but stopped before two months were out. Why, do you suppose? If it were Toronto . . ."

Before he could finish, his wife blew up. "Disgusting! I've had it with that talk! Canada again! Enough of your goddamned Canada! I had to wait three whole years, and once the electricity went out, and the water too, and the wind was blowing so hard the air filled with dust and the windows were rattling away, but you, you were in Canada, probably dancing disco." She flung out an arm and smashed a drinking glass.

Zhao Xiaoqiang froze in utter terror, as if his hybrid goldfish had suddenly turned into sea turtles. He realized then that while his well-meaning wife had never believed certain rumors about his philandering in Canada, at the subconscious level she still could not rule out the possibility that he really was guilty of such heinous deeds.

An influential personage in City V offered a few opinions of his own after hearing Zhu Shendu's report and later reiterated essentially the same opinions at several meetings. His remarks were temperate and carefully worded. He said we should still unite with certain comrades who have expressed incorrect views; we must observe policy guidelines.

They are still good comrades; they are still patriotic. After all, they did come back. And even if they hadn't, they could still be patriots, for aren't many overseas Chinese still our friends? We must allow their thinking a certain transformation process. We must be patient. If they don't come to understand in one month, we can wait two months. If they don't come around in a year, we can wait two! Why should the proletariat fear the bourgeoisie? Why should the East fear the West? Why should socialism fear capitalism? I see no call for alarm. We have great strength. The government and the army are in our hands. We must clarify what is right and wrong and unite with these comrades. We must even unite with Chiang Chingkuo. He is welcome to come back for a look around, and if he wants to return to Taiwan afterward, then fine. Of course, none of this has come about by chance. The more we open to the outside world, the clearer and stronger our limits must be."

These temperate and carefully worded remarks were passed on to every Party group in a way that stressed repeatedly that there was no call, no call for alarm, there was absolutely no call for alarm, no call whatsoever for alarm." The hope that alarm would not prevail was undoubtedly sincere, but objectively speaking, each "There's no call for alarm" added a certain measure of alarm, though no one could figure out exactly why.

Experiencing the greatest difficulties were the bathhouse attendants. Even in the eight decade of the twentieth century the vast majority of Chinese homes, including those in major cities, had no bathing facilities of their own. The bathrooms in some apartments did have bathtubs, but because there was no hot water, they were useless, so virtually everyone bathed at a bathhouse. With the increase in population and a decrease in the number of bathhouses, caused by low receipts, the bathing situation grew even tighter. Bathhouse hours were extended. Most bathhouses in City V were open from 7:00 A.M. to 10:00 P.M., fifteen hours a day. Ever since the Zhu-Zhao conflict had begun and then intensified, and ever since the temperate and carefully worded instructions had come around, bathhouses had begun to consider the question of choosing sides. Three generations of Zhus were as much the trusted authority on bathhouses in the city as Lu Ban on blacksmithing, carpentry, and masonry or Kafka for budding writers of the eighties. When the conflict became known, the Refreshing Bathhouse posted the following notice:

"In keeping with the needs of the masses and the customs of our forefathers, this bathhouse has upheld evening bathing for decades. We hereby solemnly proclaim that our daily business hours are 4:30 P.M. to midnight, and that we will not follow the wicker path of morning bathing."

The mistake of writing "wicker" for "wicked" notwithstanding, the Refreshing Bathhouse's notice had a certain taking-the-bull-by-the-horns decisiveness. The manager of the Refreshing Bathhouse felt a definite satisfaction upon posting the notice, as if he'd thrown a cheap punch in someone else's fight, or as if he'd seen Zhao Xiaoqiang suffer a defeat, even though he hadn't the faintest idea who Zhao Xiaoqiang was. It wasn't long before several other bathhouses adopted similar measures.

One of Li Lili's good friends worked in the newly built suburban Modern Bathhouse, which, as a result of Li Lili's powerful influence, took a stand of its own in posting the following:

"In order to raise people's level of consumption and promote the modernization of bathing, starting next week our daily hours will change to 3:00 A.M. to 11:00 A.M. After 11:00 A.M. bathing will stop and yogurt will be sold here instead."

92

The bathhouse was attacked from all sides, particularly by its fellow bathhouses, but the manager of the Modern Bathhouse felt more and more that he was on the forefront of a modern trend. He had his own interests as well, and he received some letters of support.

One old man called Zhao Xiaoqiang on the phone to say that what the Modern Bathhouse was doing was not right, just you watch; he took a full minute to say those twelve words, then hung up. Zhao Xiaoqiang didn't know whether to laugh or cry. What did the Modern Bathhouse have to do with him anyway?

What's more, he had his own problems. To bathe or not to bathe? If so, when? Everyone, including "influential personages," was convinced that Zhao Xiaoqiang was patriotic, but actually he had thought longingly of Canada when he came home to the inconvenience of bathing in China. Of course, he firmly believed that with the realization of the four modernizations the prospect of everyone's being able to bathe conveniently was not illusion. Once people had bathing facilities in their homes, it was essential that they be able to bathe in the morning, at noon, in the evening, once again before going to bed (when necessary), upon coming home after having been out on a windy day, when soaked with sweat on a hot summer day, or on any other number of other occasions, all without the necessity of analysis or debate. How had he fallen into the bath time debate now, when he hadn't even installed a homemade shower.

On February 14 at 7:45 P.M., at the height of the storm that had taken the whole city, he went to the Refreshing Bathhouse for a bath. It was already disastrously crowded, and he had to wait fifteen minutes before he was led by an attendant over to a smelly wicker basket and able to undress and get into the bath. When people are dirty, they don't care if the water is dirty, for dirty water can also wash one clean.

He was relaxed and content as he finished his bath. He felt like a new man. Coming out of the bathhouse, he bought melon seeds and a stick of candied haws filled with bean paste from a vendor. Eating them as he walked, he took in deep breaths of night air which already had a hint of spring to it and felt even more refreshed.

The next morning someone asked him whether it was true that he had bathed the night before, and when he admitted that he had, he was asked whether he had changed his mind about morning bathing. He said that he had said one *could* bathe in the morning, and that he had never said one could *only* bathe in the morning, and that he had never given an iron-clad guarantee that he bathed only in the morning and not at night or at some other time of the day. Moreover, he had never been opposed to bathing at times other than the morning. His questioner smiled and winked and said, "Anyway, you're of the morning bathing faction, *most* of what you've supported in the past has been morning bathing, your main thrust is morning bathing. How can you not admit what you yourself have said?"

Zhao Xiaoqiang picked up on the insulting tone of the question. He reddened slightly and said with great restraint, "Of course one can bathe in the morning, what of it?" But he felt that he was only falling in deeper. A trap?

Then he received a phone call from Yu Qiuping. "This is Xiao Yu," she said warmly. "Venerable Zhu is very happy. We know that you've used a concrete action to correct your mistake, and we approve. Come over to Venerable Zhu's when you're free, why don't you? He said he'll treat you to some genuine Ningxia wolfberry wine."

He didn't say anything.

That night Li Lili, tearful with the anguish of defeat, went to Zhao Xiaoqiang. "They're all saying that you've changed course, but I don't believe it! I argued with them

94

and nearly came to blows. I said you weren't that kind of person. You must tell me. Did you go to the Refreshing Bathhouse for a bath at night?"

Zhao Xiaoqiang felt that to answer such a question would be insane at the least. He was increasingly aware that the metaphysics of insanity could not be treated by propagating dialectics but with medications like chlorpromazine. He hung his head and said nothing.

Li Lili misunderstood his gesture. Brushing away his tears, he said, "It's true! How could you be so stupid? If you went back to that shitty bathhouse for a thousand evening baths, you still wouldn't be accepted! Why are you so afraid to be called unorthodox? Being different from everyone else—that's where a person's value lies. Why are you so intent on giving up, fitting in?"

"Have you . . . bathed . . . lately?" As soon as he asked the question, Zhao Xiaoqiang realized how foolish it had been. Li Lili was wearing a fashionable sweater and a cream-colored down jacket, but his body odor had already made it clear that he hadn't bathed in a long, long time.

Li Lili left, greatly distressed. Informants came nonstop as usual. One brought a provincial-level policy publication with an article on how only greater national spirit could bring about greater international spirit. The article said that cloth shoes had become all the rage in North America, yet certain Chinese insisted on wearing leather shoes, when actually leather shoes had come form the West and were already passé there; nowadays in the West Chinese cloth shoes were in, and under no circumstances can we blindly imitate foreign tastes.

The article went on to give the example of "Hollywood" coming to China to buy films. They saw several so-called new-wave films but passed them all by, because things that are considered new in China are old hat over there. Finally they chose only *The Petty Official* and paid a lot of money for it.

The more Zhao Xiaoqiang read, the more confused he became. Was the article criticizing following the West or advocating it? Did it want people to follow the example of foreigners, or was it opposing the blind imitation of foreign tastes?

Moreover, he had strong doubts about the reliability of such information. After all, he had lived in Canada for three years and had traveled to places like Miami in the States. People wore Chinese cloth shoes in the States because there were all kinds of people, all kinds of shoes, and all kinds of people wearing all kinds of shoes in the States. Just as there were people in the States who practiced *taijiquan* and yoga, who shaved their heads and became monks, or who, to this day, still waved photos of Kang Sheng and Zhang Chunqiao and sold "Criticize Lin Biao, Criticize Confucius" pamphlets. As for proclaiming that Chinese cloth shoes were all the rage in North America, he truly did not know whether the news was suspect or whether some mental function of his own had started to go.

His informants said that in the end the article was still obliquely referring to the bathing dispute, that it was criticizing Zhao Xiaoqiang without naming names. When Zhao Xiaoqiang heard "without naming names," he panicked. Was the article really criticizing him? He was in no position to find out, and he had no way to explain or vindicate himself. The friends who cared about him most were the most insistent that he was the one being criticized, but he could not remember ever having committed the crime of belittling cloth shoes or Henan opera. He'd rather they'd gone ahead and named names. That way, if he'd been criticized, then he'd been criticized, and if he hadn't, he hadn't.

A few days later, a national health-care publication

published an article that discussed how one's life-style should have Chinese characteristics. No one came to show it to him; Zhao Xiaoqiang discovered it on his own. When he finished reading it, his heart was pounding. Was it, too, directed at him? What was all this publicity about?

An older cousin in another town wrote and said, "Xiaoqiang, for the past few years everything has gone your way, but it can't go on like that. A few setbacks are perfectly natural, even good for you. I mean it."

Zhao Xiaoqiang felt as though he'd been put on a gyroscope and was spinning ever faster despite himself. Why did all disputes, meaningful and meaningless, become, in the end, interpersonal, dog-eat-dog struggles for advantage? Why did such disputes force one into metaphysics and absolutes? Why was it that once a dispute had taken that turn, it stuck like glue, inescapable, unshakable?

He asked his wife, but she had no answers. Then suddenly word came that someone had said that a morning bath had to be tried at least once. All smiles, Li Lili came to see him, bearing two bottles of Qingdao beer and a pound of pig's ears. Someone else phoned with congratulations. But he only felt worse. Even snuggled into bed at night, the young couple still found themselves talking about that infernal dispute with Zhu Shendu. As soon as the subject was broached, he found himself short of breath, hoarse, and barely able to speak, his heart palpitating wildly, the very signs of . . . my God!

Perhaps everything would be better tomorrow, just as, when one wakes from a drunk, the sky is clear, the water is clear, everything is settled, and a quarrel, no matter how violent, is resolved. Ah, tomorrow!

The Heat Waves of Summer

The last minute, or the last ten thousand years, are all
irretrievably past and gone, equally lost in history.
Thus we say, every moment is ten thousand years.

The heat that summer was killing. Birds dropped
dead from the sky. Cricket cages burst into flames from the
heat of the sun. An evening paper reported that one cricket
particularly imbued with Liberation Consciousness committed self-immolation to protest its man-made confinement.
Possibly one of the most reliable pieces of news that this particular newspaper had reported that whole year.

People got all worked up by the heat. They spent
their time calculating the average income of the population.
They said that in the 1960s, our GNP was about the same as
Japan's, but that under the Tang dynasty,[1] our GNP was
around sixty times that of Japan, if not seventy times. People
recalled that as early as the 1950s, a scientist had figured out
that according to the laws of the conversion of energy, most
of our northern territories could produce twenty thousand
jin[2] of rice per mu.[3] Once this was achieved, we would again
be Number One under Heaven. The bronze chariot and

1. A.D. 618–907.
2. Equivalent to 0.5 kilo.
3. 0.667 hectare.

horses excavated near Xi'an were proof that we had led the world in smelting, chariot making, and horse breeding. That is, until the Monkey took over as Bi-Ma-Wen, Supervisor of the Celestial Stables, with a title equivalent to deputy department chief.[4]

At our study sessions, we went over these rousing facts, current and historical. We declared that once we smashed the socialist "iron rice bowl" and the "big cooking pot," our productivity would go up nine times. The basis for this calculation was a popular saying familiar to every man, woman, and child: "One billion people, nine-tenths talking, only one-tenth toiling." We now figured that if the other 900 million also started working, even if they worked only eight hours a day, we could institute the five-hour day and lead the world. People complained that now that the bus dispatchers had gotten a raise, the conductors refused to work. Last night, Little Zhang was on the No. 358 bus. He went up to the conductor, cash in hand, and was practically shooed away. Robbed of the chance to fulfill his civic duties, Little Zhang was indignant: " 'Take class struggle as the key link,'[5] that's what the Chinese deserve. Send 5 percent of them to labor-reform, and see if it doesn't work magic."

Everybody worried themselves sick over the fate of the nation and the luck of the people and labor productivity and discipline and efficiency and percentages and values and so on. They worried so much their teeth started falling out. But then they conceded "It's been better the last couple of years." Then Lao Dong added: "It's getting better indeed. If only it had been like this all those past years. . . ." "Bullshit!" everybody shouted at her, and then sighed in unison:

4. A pun. In Chinese folklore, the monkey is said to be able to ward off disease from horses. Also, Mao had referred to himself as the Monkey.
5. Quotation from Chairman Mao.

"Might as well spit it out, what do you lose? Though having said it, what do you gain?"

And having said it, they ran for their lives—it was twenty minutes before closing time and all the offices had emptied. To avoid the bus jams, one had to get to work late and leave early. Everybody being of the same mind, the high tide of the bus jams moved accordingly, getting later and later in the mornings and earlier and earlier in the afternoons. My predecessor, the highly myopic old Mr. Du, had wanted to rectify this situation. He sat in the gatehouse himself to check on late arrivals, and even moved himself into the big common office, just to keep an eye on everyone. He set himself against the masses and thus incurred their collective wrath. In the whole of our bureau, he was the only one forced to retire on the dot of the hour that he reached the retirement age as reckoned by his horoscope. After all, people said, if he wants to be so particular . . .

The papers, meanwhile, reported that ten-thousand-yuan peasant households were buying pianos. And cars. And airplanes. Maybe even atom bombs. Scenes of peasants' motorbike brigades appeared on TV. A young girl made enough money by selling tea-flavored eggs to fly to the U.S. to study. Bought her own airplane ticket. Our people worked themselves into a fury. After all, we are the ones engaged in highly complex mental labor. Why was it nowadays that we eggheads were making less than people selling eggs? Someone raised the further question: when He was alive, the brainier you were the more reactionary you were; now that He is gone, it seems the brainier you are the poorer you are. Lao Dong stamped her foot in exasperation. "Why is it," she cried, "that some people are like ginseng—the older the better, while we are like turnips, the older the bitterer?" Everybody cheered her on. Old Mrs. Dong stamped again and made a hole in the planks of the floor. Out jumped a plump, white mouse. Everybody laughed merrily and said living standards have indeed gone up. See, even the mice have become plump and white, as if they were fed on baby formula.

The engine roared as the people seeing him off said their last good-byes. He acted polite, turning on his smile right and left for all his friends. All this was conducted on a subconscious level, just as on that occasion fifteen years ago, when he knew he was drunk but still remained very much aware that, as host, the last thing he needed was to appear drunk. So he had preserved his genial smile and made sure not one of his guests had felt neglected. He had seen his guests off, and then walked down three blocks, across two crossings, through a flow of bicycles and cars. Yet later, he had no idea how he had done it.

He felt his whole body glowing, abandoned to a mixture of sweetness and pain. He felt like a fish, proud and free. He felt like a fish boiled or fried, with a sauce blended of vinegar and bean paste and pepper heated in vegetable oil to 150 degrees and poured over its body. The brightness from the huge windows of the airport dazzled the eyes, like waves brought to a boiling point by the sun. A babel of sounds, sharp and penetrating, hit him like a rolling tide, and devoured him in its embrace. The noise was deafening: the air control tower seemed to swell, to disintegrate, to be shuddering its way right into the terminal. Airplanes on the runway raised their necks expectantly, yet completely devoid of hope. Meanwhile an incoming airplane seemed to swoop down maliciously. In the middle of the confusion, he could still make out that soft, innocent voice, like a whisper in his ear: "Am I not good?"

The whisper was eluding him, yet it kept reverberating. Her enormous eyes unnerved and frightened him. No Chinese woman had such enormous eyes. They were like a pair of ordinary eyes with the eyelids forced apart. And the dark black translucent irises seemed to go on expanding insistently. These eyes stared out stubbornly, and—he would add—vacantly.

I relayed the instructions of the top brass. July 8 was set aside as the beginning of the Month of Reform. Things would begin to Happen. Loosening up. Contracts signed. Responsibility System. Stocks and percentages. Hiring and firing. Piecework wages and profit sharing. Bonuses. Basic wages. The Third Wave brings old China a new chance. Computerized checks on work attendance. Bold experiments needed. Pioneering leadership in demand. New faces, new outlooks expected. We're on the verge of a big step forward . . .

Increased fervor, brought to a boiling pitch, as if the skies were raining stuffed buns and cream cakes, as if our rivers were swollen with liquor and mao-tai. We were inundated by new information beyond our wildest imaginings. New slogans exploded around us: "One-Track Mind Bent on Enrichment." "Work Hard, Spend Fast." "Jump Right into the Third Wave." New measures will be taken, like measuring all the staff for new suits, complete with jackets and ties. New companies will be formed, with no offices, equipment, or capital—just an Information Service Center. Information brings wealth, multiplying many times over. New work system to be installed like the 3/3 System, with one-third of the staff on duty, one-third on tours of inspection here and abroad, and one-third in business to make profits. Best Wishes for Enormous Profits! Glory to the Highest Consumer! This is the currency of the times! What are you talking about? "Thrift and economy" my foot! Downright reactionary! If we had converted our bureau into a pig farm, we would have made big profits long ago. No, pig raising is too dirty. Raising flies is better. We could breed the flies needed

102

by scientists all over the world. Great, it would be a pioneering effort on a global scale. You should have a bronze statue erected in your honor, you standing upright, your hands outstretched, your palms overrun with flies. Scientists and scientific institutions all over the world, in biology, ecology, genetics, genetic engineering, medicine, and biochemistry, would all order our flies. Our prices would be reasonable, each internationally standardized fly would cost $1.50, or 2.5 deutsche marks.

She was dressed in black velvet, with a white silk scarf draped around her neck. Chekhov had a character called Nina in one of his plays who always dressed in black. When asked why she always dress in black, she answered: "I am commiserating with life, I am so unhappy . . ."

"Our leadership should be democratically elected. Appointments from above simply eliminate the best and brightest and leave us with the dregs. No leader will voluntarily acknowledge that anybody else is, or ever will be, better than himself. This alone is enough to ensure a genetic degeneration—what you might call the weasel breeding rats—each generation worse than the previous . . ." Xiao Zhang spoke with conviction, his eloquence enhanced by his Hubei accent.

More and more people brought Xiao Zhang to my attention. Xiao Zhang is a capable man, they said, cut out to be an official. He too was already hinting: "Now if *I* were governor of the province . . ."

"Of course we want to elect a capable man," everybody kept saying, "a new-style leader who will lead us into modernization, who'll make us rich. . . . We'd be fools if we let him slip through our fingers. . . . But who's the right man?"

"Who? Everybody should have a chance! Didn't Napoleon say that the soldier who doesn't want to be general isn't a good soldier? The cadre who doesn't want to be a top official isn't a good cadre! Now that we are in the Year of Reform, and specifically in the Month of Reform, each and everyone should come up with a Program. Those good-for-nothings with no inclination, sense, or ability should clear out. They can peddle silk stockings from Hong Kong!"

"You don't know what you are talking about! It is precisely the peddlars who are most Reform-minded!" There is a burst of laughter.

"Come now, Xiao Zhang, what if you make a start? Suppose you run for election? Now, if you had a contract to run our bureau, what would you do?"

"Don't start with me. First let the others tell what *they'll* do." The fellow seems to have something up his sleeve.

"Xiao Zhang is right. Everybody should compete!" The young fellows were getting excited. "People who don't have the guts to compete should be kicked out."

"I just won't compete. If I'm kicked out, I'll go begging in the streets," Lao Dong said. There was another burst of laughter.

After several rounds of verbal sparring, Xiao Zhang exclaimed vehemently: "If I contracted to run this place, first of all the budget would have to be tripled. Secondly, the staff should be cut by two-thirds. The old, the unruly, the lazy— you in particular," and he pointed a finger viciously at me, "must all go. And once you're out, I wash my hands of you all. Alive or dead, you're no longer my concern. Finally, I must have Power, power over finances, power over personnel, and power to decide policy. Everything must be solely in my hands. As far as personnel issues are concerned, let me make this clear: those who side with me will be promoted, and those who oppose me will be cut down. Otherwise, where would the authority be that goes with leadership? How would we increase efficiency? Take salaries, for instance; it must be entirely up to me to decide who gets what. Otherwise, who would be grateful to me? Who would exert himself on my behalf?"

At least half of his audience clapped. Some even shouted: "We want Xiao Zhang!" "Give Xiao Zhang a contract!" "Let Xiao Zhang lead us into prosperity!"

I was totally at a loss. Perhaps I really should yield my office to one who is worthier, and let Xiao Zhang have a try? He might change things for the better. But why did he have to act so aggressive, showing his muscle?

The airplane roared into the air, and the horizon reeled. He knew that all this has become irrevocably part of the past. He parted, a lonely island. He parted from her as he would from the dead. What is the past? The grave and the cross.

As he shook hands with those seeing him off, she gave him a hug. He became aware of her face, the skin rough and cold, the cheekbones stiff and angular. This was her fate. She was doomed to a bitter fate and would never know a better one. This was more painful than any dainty softness. The pain was like a fire, burning down buildings, burning the hair, burning the heart. Only a pile of debris was left behind, already turning cold though still smoldering.

And then over the debris, over the cloven land, new cities were built up, with dazzling lights, and gorgeous stores, and heavily made-up women, and smoke from grilled meat, and singing which sounded more like weeping, and vast arrays of goods for sale, and a mad, mad rhythm, and danger of robbery, and the trap of desires, and bodies increasingly exposed with souls increasingly indiscernible.

How are you?

How are you?

At the revolving door of a five-star hotel, they greeted each other. He knew nothing of this city, nor of this hotel, nor of this person. Perhaps his attraction lay precisely in the fact that he was a stranger. He was like an arrival from outer space, staring and gaping.

She looked at him curiously, stupidly, sadly.

He shuddered.

The leaders argued through the night without coming to a decision. But the rumor spread that Xiao Zhang was going to take over.

We were flooded by letters of complaint: Xiao Zhang had stolen paint from the carpenter's workshop. Xiao Zhang had smashed records of *Swan Lake* when he was a Red Guard. Xiao Zhang was trying to go abroad and had written to people in the U.S. Xiao Zhang had once bribed a driver and taken his whole family to a scenic spot 125 kilometers away.

We were also flooded by letters of recommendation and praise. Xiao Zhang is a pioneering spirit. As early as 1968 he had said the countryside should be run on the contract system. Once, during a fire in the conference room, Xiao Zhang had very opportunely poured five basins of water on a smoldering sofa and emptied the contents of the spittoon over the head of the section chief. Xiao Zhang had both professional abilities and organizational skills, a rare cadre who met every requirement. Xiao Zhang is the rare thousand-li thoroughbred waiting to be spotted by someone with the discrimination and decision of a modern Bole.[6]

Lost in a maze of indecision and confusion, people

6. Historical figure renowned for expertise in judging horses, now a metaphor for someone who recognizes and promotes talent.

weighed the pros and cons of Xiao Zhang's taking office. Which was a safer bet, being pro-Zhang or anti-Zhang? And what exactly were X and Y up to? Were they making a pretense of opposing Zhang but really supporting him? Or making a pretense of supporting him but really opposing him? Or supporting him and opposing him at the same time? And was this wisdom or downright unethical, this sort of maneuvering with a foot in each camp and leaving a back door open just in case? People started to worry whether or not they would be appointed once the contract system was in operation. Some felt that this was the time to offer Xiao Zhang some potency-enhancing Chinese herbal medicine, while others eloquently praised the system from which they had reaped such benefits. Some started visiting retired leaders who still had some influence, bemoaning their impending fate at the hands of Xiao Zhang. The former leaders would ask: "But Xiao Zhang has not taken over yet, isn't that so?" "True, but he's already made us feel the pinch; once he's installed, it will be worse for our old bones." Some went to Xiao Zhang, offering him advice and a list of connections, somewhat similar to the traditional "Mandarin's Life Preserver."[7] Some announced that they would commit suicide if not rehired, and started to write out and Xerox their suicide notes. Some made public statements for Xiao Zhang's and my benefit: "It's okay if I'm not rehired. I've long lost interest in this job, no bonuses and no chance to go abroad. . . . Who wants to hang on, anyway? But there's one thing. If you don't rehire Lao Li either, then it's okay. Or if you rehire me without rehiring Lao Li, that's okay too. But, if you rehire Lao Li without rehiring me, you'll never hear the end of it. It will be a case of sticking the white blade in and pulling it out

7. A set of verses listing the local magnates, whom a newly arrived official could not afford to offend.

red. Oh, I won't stick it into other people. Just into my own breast. You can't object to that, can you?"

Five days later, Xiao Zhang couldn't hold out any longer. He handed in a formal report: "I am determined not to be a leading official, not at any price! Please don't nominate me to any leading position. I have a big mouth, but I can't tackle real problems. Please don't be affected by the talk going around. My appointment to a leadership position will inflict irreparable damage on the people, the country, and myself."

Xiao Zhang was more outspoken in private conversation. "Bullshit! All this show of concern for the nation and the people, all this talk of Reform! No one will lift a finger for Reform when it comes to the crunch. All of them are waiting for the skies to drop meat-stuffed buns. Dining off the north wind is more bloody likely."

The leadership finally decided against Xiao Zhang's appointment. They decided to renew mine.

They held a big ceremony to confer the certificate of appointment on me. Actually, I had been heading this bureau for the last two years.

A dazzling world of luxury. A brighly lit street lined with stores with extravagant displays, like a celestial capital. All the people carried heavy hearts under their respectable clothing. At one store, all the items on display were spotlighted in a tempting red glow, with staggering figures on their price tags. Such perfect service, every need taken care of, regulations for every detail.

How do you feel then, strolling through such a place?

Satisfaction, as if being massaged, as if having my body licked by my pet dog. As if even my smile had acquired elegance. I felt myself wafting down like a petal and being covered by petals.

I felt it was more than I could bear, my digestive system

seemed to be too much for me. I felt a swelling, and congestion, and heartburn. I felt like an overloaded boat slowly sinking.

I felt angry, humiliated, like a beggar. Like a man under arrest, I was ashamed, as if I were a prodigal son who had sold the family heirloom.

Getting to the bottom of the question, it was just loneliness. The more active, the more successful, the lonelier. Can the relationship between man and the environment, between man and the earth, and between man and the clan, can these relationships be so fragile?

A light rain began to fall. They huddled together in the entrance of a store. The city seemed quiet and refined. Even cars were driven carefully. They passed the stores, one after another. False hair, jewelry, suitcases of all sizes, cosmetics. And then they passed an empty alley littered with plastic garbage bags. The little alley was dark and gave out a strong smell. They walked into a white building. White round tables, white stools, a sheath of wall-length mirrors. They ordered coffee. Turkish or Italian? the waiter asked. With a dash of brandy imported from South Africa? The United Nations was imposing sanctions on South Africa for apartheid.

He gazed at the trees' shadows outside the window, the flow of traffic, the pedestrians rushing by, each with his own problems within his breast.

"Once upon a time, there were two naughty children, a boy and a girl, and a famous restaurant was named after the two of them . . ."

"When I was little, I was naughty. My aunt often scolded me, sometimes she hit me. My aunt had a yellow-haired dog. One day I smeared its snout with red paint . . ."

He seemed uninterested. "Let us go, I am tired," he said.

Formerly, I had been the leading cadre. Now, I was supposed to have a contract to run the office, a contract for three years. So be it. I was also informed that all power was delegated to me, what is referred to as "the power of life and death."

The first problem I came up against was, "Whom do I rehire, and whom, by default, fire?"

The person I was most reluctant to rehire was Lao Zhao. He was an "operator," always flitting from one home to another, leaving gifts or invitations, adept at the new science of "networking," quick to decode the significance of "name lists," and knowing exactly who was worth "cultivating." But when it came to a real issue, he never had an opinion; he would refuse to get involved, and never lifted a finger to do a spot of work. On the other hand, he always had to be top dog, was touchy in the extreme and good at sabotage. For instance, on the simple matter of providing instant coffee for the office staff, Lao Zhao turned down the corners of his mouth contemptuously: "Taking coffee doesn't necessarily mean opening up, and not taking coffee doesn't necessarily mean conservatism and rigidity." Out of respect for his opinion, we decided to cancel the free coffee proposal. But then he said: "You can't say that we are upholding the national tradition just by not drinking coffee; but you also can't say that by drinking coffee, we are worshipers of everything foreign." When we tried to pin down exactly what he wanted, he said he had no opinion: "Let the masses decide."

Realistically I had no choice except to hire him. Otherwise, an avalanche would descend on me. Certain members of the leadership and certain influential figures would immediately sympathize with him. I would be considered intolerant of dissidence, putting private grudges before the general interest and I don't know what. I would be the public enemy. Xiao Zhang and his buddies would get all the wrong signals, draw all the wrong conclusions, and scheme against Lao Zhao more feverishly than ever. That bunch always hurts more than they help. And Lao Dong and her buddies would also get all the wrong signals, draw all the wrong conclusions. They would rush to apply for transfers, for time off, for hospitalization, and then the letters would begin flowing in for my impeachment. The last thing I wanted was to antagonize that crowd.

The second person I was reluctant to rehire was Lao Dong. During the Cultural Revolution, she had produced a supplement to her files, certifying her poor peasant background for three generations, and asserting that she herself had been a child laborer. Last year, she suddenly produced another certificate with proof that she had graduated from night school by the 1950s with a degree in higher education. She demanded promotion as a higher intellectual. To reinforce her demand, she wept and screamed and poured a bottle of mosquito repellant down her throat right before our eyes. Finally even Xiao Zhang was impressed. "Okay, okay, let her have it. Let's hold our noses and vote her an associate researcher. . . . I have only one thing to say, we must pass a special regulation for Lao Dong: for every day she comes to work, one yuan will be deducted from her paycheck, and for every day she misses work, she will be rewarded ten fen; if she doesn't show up from one end of the year to the next, she will be rewarded as a model worker, we'll pin the big red paper flower on her breast, and give her a bonus."

Xiao Zhang, of course, was exaggerating, but Lao Dong was a pain. She always brought mischief in her wake. That's a fact.

I had no choice but to rehire her. Otherwise, she would turn the whole place upside down. Besides, her maternal uncle was universally acknowledged as an upright figure, and a big shot, too. This highly respected figure had married an illiterate country woman with bound feet, five years older than himself. Still they were a loving couple, respecting each other like honored guests, as the saying goes. How can one have the temerity to shove her aside, the maternal niece of such a venerable figure! If I don't give them "face," it will be seen as thumbing my nose at the masses.

And thus, I could not rehire the ones I wanted to, but was afraid not to rehire the ones I wanted to get rid of. This so-called power of life and death I now possessed just made things worse. It put me on the spot; I didn't have a vague "leadership" to pin the blame on. Don't push a man too hard, people kept reminding me. Even I kept reminding myself.

A telegram arrived. My old friend A.K. had died of cancer. A bolt out of the blue. Like a smoothly gliding airplane bursting into flames with no warning.

He had been such a good sport during those years when we were undergoing "mass struggle." He had made doggerel verses and sung, "Meeting my executioners, I drink a last bowl of wine from the hands of my mother,"[8] and danced the "Loyalty to Mao" dance. He had learned the carpenter's craft. When the Cultural Revolution was over and he returned to his post, the old carpenter of the workshop sighed: "I never had an apprentice that smart. Cut out to be a first-rate carpenter. And now he's back to being a lousy cadre. What a waste!"

Could it be possible that an airplane flying in the air would suddenly explode for no reason at all?

This is an enormous swing, skirts billowing, swallows flying. This is a huge sailing boat, surging ahead to the sound of a bugle. This is a punctured parachute, I want to soar on the wings of the wind, but the flying general crashed down from the skies.

This is a complete mistake. He shouldn't have asked,

8. From *The Red Lantern*, one of Madame Mao's eight model operas.

"Would you like a drink?" He realized only later that such an invitation at such a late hour implied intimacy.

The city was reeling, the floodlights were entangled in each other, the pavement was rising, was standing up perpendicularly, was swaying over our heads. Shadows flitted here and there, sounds of laughter floated in the air, a babble of voices exuded the exuberance of youth. A dizziness without smoke, a scent without flowers, a palpitating of the heart without reason. Like sitting in bumper cars. Mutual strangers, wary of each other, trying to avoid contact, but eventually crashing into each other. You try to avoid contact, yet anticipate crashing into each other. Why do people want to crash into complete strangers?

But she was so lonely. Lonely as a withered blade of grass in a garden plot. Lonely as a gray magpie in the snow. Loneliness planted white hairs on her head, first one, then another. As the poet had said, "white hairs three thousand feet long," and desolation lingering on without end.

And she was helpless, like an airplane falling, like a boat sinking.

A white cottage, with white frescoes on the walls, and a white fireplace. Why was it necessary to throw in a few logs in summer? Well, at night, a chilly breeze blows in from the sea, and one yearns for the crackling of firewood, the sight of flames leaping and dancing. As if that were all the sound and all the movement left in the world.

While the city, on the other hand, was a medley of the sights and sounds of pleasure and luxury. Could it be that he and she were like beggars? In the choking, evil-smelling smog, the roar of rock 'n' roll thundered in their ears, thumping at their hearts, gripping at their bowels, pounding their jaws, shattering their teeth.

In the roaring noise, he could hardly open his eyes from

tiredness. As in a trance, he felt himself being pounded, and kneaded, and crashed into.

Thirty years ago, he might have started dancing. He would have responded to this loneliness, this warmth, this roaring, this strangeness, he would have embraced this strangeness.

No, an airplane had no business exploding in midair.

I was not totally resourceless.

"All pessimism, all theories of stagnation and helplessness are entirely wrong." The great leader Mao Zedong had said so. But it seems that people have stopped reciting quotations from the little *Red Book*. His sayings were rarely quoted on the front pages of the papers nowadays. Well, here today, gone tomorrow. May his venerable soul rest in peace.

I had started a Center with a production line and a service line, making ourselves part of the third industry. One-fourth of the bureau staff was transferred to this perilous and tricky job, which was not without its own rewards, however. This meant that I had cut the staff by one-fourth. Everybody knew what was going on, but I still kept repeating: this is not staff reduction, this is not staff reduction. I repeated it until my lips were bruised and others' ear overgrown with callus. If I did not go through these motions, this new state of things would not be accepted.

Parents often tell their young children, when forcing medicine down their throats: "It's not medicine. It's candy," or "It's fruit juice." But the young children whimper, "It is medicine."

Our adults are more childish than children. Such good people they are!

After a lot of Sturm und Drang, finally two individuals were not rehired. One was Xiao Liu. He had handed in his resignation three times in a row. He had complained that there's nothing to look forward to: no rise to officialdom, no

114

fame, no profits. Besides, he was busy planning his wedding. "I might as well quit and go into business. I have the connections. We can buy and sell TV receivers, a cool one-thousand-yuan profit for every deal." Xiao Zhang was impressed. China's future depends on the likes of Xiao Liu, he said.

The other was Lao Zhang. She had been on sick leave for the last three years. In less than six months, she would have reached the age of retirement. To make the non-rehiring more palatable, we promoted her to deputy department chief status and then announced a temporary non-rehirement, reserving for her all the privileges of department chief status.

And thus the broiling summer came and went. As did the Month of Reform and the Season of Reform. People started returning from their seaside holidays in Beidahe, Qingdao, Dalian, and the Sunny Island in the Songhua River near Harbin. They commended my decisiveness, congratulated me for having made a big step forward. My colleagues nodded in approval: "You haven't done too badly, heh?" At some meetings, Lao Zhao criticized me for acting too slowly on Reform. At other meetings he criticized me for being too precipitous. He also pointed out that the windowpanes were not properly wiped and that the drivers of the office cars should not be fitted with uniforms at public expense. At the same time he said that the drivers must change the way they dress, that it was not just a matter of clothes. . . . Lao Dong requested a formal audience. Since Lao Zhang could be promoted to department chief level, she argued, she herself must be likewise honored. She stated in no uncertain terms that she expects deputy department chief status when she reaches the age of retirement in a year's time.

A couple of departments made some routine personnel changes. Otherwise all the departments were now on contracts and run by their previous leaders; the previous staff members were rehired on the same principle. Terms of office and terms of rehiring were announced. Speeches were made about raising efficiency and smashing the big cooking pot and the iron rice bowls and all that.

And then things were back to normal.

Articles appeared in the papers, offering different opinions. Some said the iron rice bowl was the fruit of our long struggle and should not be done away with in one fell swoop. Others said that promoting Western-style suits was a case of overconsumption. Still others said that the spirit of frugality—"new for three years, old for three years, patched up and lasting another three years"—would live on forever.

The cicadas slowed down their singing. There were fewer staccatos, just one long, drawn-out sigh, hovering in the air, heard one moment and gone the next.

I can feel your closeness, your tenderness, but I do not know you.

I cannot bear to see your eyes welling up with tears. As I cannot bear to see an old man ambling on alone under the glitter and glare of a thousand lights. As I cannot bear to see a dying man playing a single melancholy tune over and over again on his violin, unable to stop.

To resist her outstretched hand, that would have been too cruel, like taking a life.

I should not have offered you a glass of orange juice. Why is it that one cannot have a glass of orange juice like that in our great motherland?

So many jokes, so many memories of childhood. Like one's first firecracker, every nerve in the body tensed in expectation, as if one were grown up and about to explode a mine in the enemy's fortress. One waits and waits, shivering in a cold sweat. But the firecracker did not explode.

The opportunity was thus missed forever.

Perhaps the world could begin again. Could we relocate the

116

Kunlun Mountains in the sea? Could we make the Arctic waters a resort for pleasure boats? Could we make the trees bear diamonds instead of fruit and sheep open their mouths and bare wolf-like fangs? Perhaps, at the moment when he and she embrace, the bells of heaven will ring and a huge turtle will appear with a picture of the Apocalypse on its back and make its way to the square in front of the parliament building, and then all binding ropes, all rules and regulations, all laws governing planets and satellites will dissolve, a burning sun will consume them and all her tears will dry up.

No.

There is only one thing left to say, acceptable to heroes and cowards alike: Let us go on with our uneventful lives.

Thus time passed. You could not tell whether it was five months or five years.

I received a flurry of funeral notices; old friends were dying one after another. One had become a vegetable due to softening of the brain. Nobody believed he would ever get well; on the other hand, nobody wished him a swift demise. He must hang on—for the sake of his privileges, at the very least. Honored the dead might be, but they can't enjoy the privileges of office. Honored the dead might be, but in this, our increasingly ancient and childish nation, they would be soon forgotten.

Without the stimulant of forgetfulness, how can we, the descendants of Emperors, survive to this day?

I went to the barber for a haircut. Waiting in a line is a good test of willpower and character. "Isn't this shop run on a contract?" I asked the barber.

"Yes," the man sighed. "Yes. Everything's on contract. Just a formality."

"Formality? A state-owned shop now leased to private individuals, and you call it a formality?"

"Everything goes on as it did in the old days."

"Aren't you paid on a piece rate? Isn't haircutting the easiest thing to reckon by piece? And hasn't the price of a haircut just doubled?"

"Piece rate my foot! What are you going to do about the old master workers? Who among the contractors dares to offend them? Your lease runs out in three years, and then what? More work, more pay? What do you know? The more you do, the more offense you give! The less you do, the more you get!"

He was full of complaints. I didn't know how much to believe.

But I myself soon came under attack in the bureau that I had contracted for. The first shot came from Xiao Zhang.

"Reform! Reform! Just talk! With all this Reform, have we seen a cent in raises? And we never get handouts, not even a fur coat. Just look at the Ministry of X, everyone on their staff got a piano!"

And thus it dawned on me that Reform meant a raise. Reform meant giving out leather shoes, brass Mongolian hot pots, refrigerators, pianos. Reform meant giving every man two wives and every woman four lovers. Reform meant no cold blasts in winter and free Popsicles in summer. Reform meant everyone gets a free trip at public expense to the United States of America, to Japan, Australia, Canada, Italy, or Switzerland, to be followed by their children and grand-children going abroad through private sponsors. Reform meant everybody opening their mouths wide and filling them incessantly with beer and mao-tai and royal jelly and fruit-flavored oxtail soup. Reform meant giving out a medium-range pistol per person. Target: the throat. Range: seventy-five millimeters. Ready, Aim, Fire.

And Xiao Zhang and his buddies were like a nestful of chicks with their beaks wide open, waiting for Reform:

118

"Why don't you Reform?" They pursued me with the question.

"Would you like anything to drink?" The waiter was the essence of politeness. Black jacket, striped pants, elegant black bow tie.

The sounds of a piano rippled through the lounge, like drops of summer rain from a black cloud, hovering undetermined in the sky.

You were also the essence of politeness, as if you had rehearsed your every move.

Soda water and punch with slices of lemon stood between him and her, as if between the North Atlantic Treaty and the Warsaw Pact nations, presumably to ensure their mutual safety.

"What is missing is only nuclear bombs hanging over our heads like chandeliers."

But she is a hopeless case, she does not understand. You know that she is wondering, "Why?"

She even said hesitatingly, "Let us break through that wall."

First break through his heart. If there were no wall and no bombs, if indeed "the world was filled with love" according to the words of the song sung by the stars of the Eastern Dance Troupe under flashing laser lights, then would it not mean another flood?

If the world was flooded with love, do you have a life jacket?

My project of a Center with a production line and services for hire had paid off. As our items of service increased, so did our income. But Xiao Zhang groaned: "The work is killing! It's killing!"

Then one day a notice arrived: dissociate yourselves from the Center. More notices followed. Taxes in arrear. A percentage of profits will be deducted. Auditing problems discovered; manager of the Center will be put under investigation. Center will either immediately clear off the premises, or pay a 260 percent rent increase. Electricity, transportation, and mailing charges of the Center will be increased by 300 percent. Reregister for a new license, or be disbanded as an illegal organization. The Center's car has been confiscated for breaking traffic rules. Owing to substandard conditions of fire-prevention equipment and poor sanitary conditions of the dining room, the Center is ordered to stop operations for an overall rectification.

And thus it happened that the Center's manager had to give a total of seventeen banquets, hosting more than two hundred honored guests. The most popular dish was "Buddha over the Wall"—signifying that even Buddha, lured by the aroma, had leapt over the monastery wall to partake of this dish. Buddha have mercy!

Then reporters came nosing around, ready to break the news of the Center's excessive wining and dining. And then it happened that the Center threw an additional five banquets for the reporters.

Never swim against the tide. I, in all my decisiveness, gave the order: "Close down the Center!" I swept aside all protests with a question: Do you want to go to jail?

"You are like a prince," she said, and then asked, "perhaps you would like to treat me to self-service breakfast?"

"An honor and a pleasure."

Politeness brings pleasure, but also exhaustion.

Her mouth was ugly, like that of a little frog. He could not bear to look at her mouth.

But her smile was sincere, and bitter in its helplessness. She ate a pear, and two slices of cheese, and even drank a big glass of cold milk. The drinks of last night were unfinished.

He had no appetite, and just called for a glass of mineral water.

120

That same night they had passed through an empty shopping mall. Groups of young people were hanging around, smoking. Did they have nothing to do? Were they waiting for world revolution? Were they sick and tired of rock 'n' roll and sex? What if they were made to sit through a political study session, or go for a stint of labor in a May 7 cadre school?

A young compatriot, in proud possession of a "Chinese Heart",[9] *collected the empty cans from the free drinks on the flight, and the plastic tableware, and free brochures in the hotel lounge, mostly illustrated ads, and all the dirty plastic bags. . . . Before he left the hotel, he also stuffed a roll of toilet paper into his suitcase.*

Another friend, though not a compatriot, unplugged the telephone and took it with him before he checked out.

More time passed. For the moment, the funeral notices had stopped. It seemed that the Angel of Death was taking a break.

All the staff, male and female alike, engaged at the Center have migrated back to their original posts.

And what about Xiao Liu, who had not been rehired? Xiao Liu had said that he would go, but actually he didn't. He took sick leave, drawing his full salary, and gave himself a long break. During this break he married and fathered a child and buried his mother (after she died, of course). He made furniture, put up wallpaper, and changed all the lights in his apartment to designer chandeliers. He had also made two visits to his home village and translated a book of psychology. Meanwhile his pals in the TV business had ended in jail. As for Xiao Liu, it was certified that he had never dabbled in profiteering. All he had done was to prattle about the grandiose prospects of such a business. During this interval—let me put it this way—during that hot summer he was

9. The words of a popular song, "My Chinese Heart."

not yet married, and now his son has eight teeth.

And what about Lao Zhang, the other staff member not rehired? The chronically ill Lao Zhang, after losing her position, regained her health miraculously. Medical certificates began to turn up stating that she was recovering by degrees, and finally announced that she was perfectly recovered, just as in the old days she had produced papers certifying that she was progressively ill, advancing to the point when she became a complete wreck.

What was to be done? Should I go on refusing to hire those two and just let them stay home, collecting their salaries?

Or should I stop their salaries, or dock their wages? First of all, the rules for such cases have not been made. And secondly, even if they were, wouldn't it be driving them to desperation?

Not to mention the fact that they themselves, their relatives, their old buddies, and their former superior officers all came to remonstrate with me: How can you deprive them of their work? they said.

Furthermore, my own term of contract had already expired, and had not been renewed. But I was not asked to step down. I guess my superior who had issued me the contract had altogether forgotten its terms.

All right, all right. I kept my cool, with a smile pasted on my lips. The eternal laws are immutable, and Xiao Liu and Lao Zhang were back at their jobs. More time passed, and Lao Zhang submitted a certificate stating that due to the delicate condition of her health, she should go on half leave. Xiao Liu submitted an application for a transfer. It turned out that all his friends in the TV business were out of jail and thriving. Xiao Zhang, however, was detained by the police for fighting in the trolley. I went to the police station to bail him out, only to have him accuse me of knuckling under to the forces of evil. Evidently he had expected me to use martial arts against the head of the police station and lay the man flat on his face.

Our bureau was allotted five new apartments. After several bouts of bloody warfare in which heads were almost cracked open, it was decided that the new apartments should go to Lao Zhao, Lao Dong, Lao Zhang, Xiao Zhang, and Xiao Liu. When they moved, I was shocked to discover that Xiao Liu, who had been loudest in complaints about his poverty, not only owned a refrigerator, a washing machine, and a color TV, but also boasted a piano and an electric guitar. His son, barely three years old, was already taking music lessons. And believe it or not, Xiao Liu drank scotch and smoked Marlboros.

Lao Dong showed up with yet another certificate, stating that not only was she descended from three generations of poor peasants and in possession of a degree in higher education, but that she *also* had blood relations in Taiwan, which entitles her to special privileges! My superiors were all breathing down my neck, telling me to give her a promotion.

Here at last was a chance to exercise Power. I put my foot down and said: No!

The summer is over. Good-bye. Have a safe trip. Perhaps we will not know each other when we meet again.

Are the heaving tides an expression of the energy of the seas? No matter how they rage, the tides will ultimately quiet down. No matter how quiet, the seas will ultimately rise up in heaving tides.

This heart of yours, which treasures peace and quiet, and still yearns for the heaving tides! A gull flew over the sea. What is it that it expects from the sea? And what is it that it rejects from the sea?

The summer will come back. The summer is just begin-

ning. The summer will not be forgotten. Since the commotion of the prelude has been played out, how can the curtain not rise on the drama proper? As you gaze at the heaving tide, you are lost in thought for this summer as you watch it slipping by.

Fine Tuning

The couple took out years and years of their savings and went and bought a twenty-inch color TV set.

Since then, television took over their lives. They spent all their spare time watching TV programs, be it advertizing or lessons in foreign languages, in Chinese chess, or accounting. They didn't even miss the diagrams on the testing screen. As they watched, they would exclaim: "Wonderful! Just wonderful! We've made a big leap in our lifestyle! These programs are so interesting! Where else can you find something entertaining and educational at the same time? With a TV set, even life without a son is all right! TV has opened up a new era in family life, a new age! TV has brought a dramatic change to our lives, to our country! We've actually realized three and a half of the Four Modernizations! The moon over China is getting rounder and rounder!" In short, that color TV set became a veritable little sun around which their lives revolved.

After six months, they began to find fault: "How come it's always the same old thing?" "How come it's advertizing again?" "Why such a long list of names at the beginning and the end?" "The double eyelids on this broadcaster are false." "That broadcaster's cheekbones are too prominent." "Oh, see how this fatty waddles!" "Look at that fake. And he thinks he looks profound!" "These clothes must be all government issued." "Nobody laughs at this comedian!" "That make-up job is terrible!" "Well, well! So now instead of foreigners kissing, we get something quintessentially Chinese: concubines and selection of imperial consorts!"

Gradually, the criticism took a sharper turn: "Pure nonsense!" "Get out of here!" "How come they can't even pronounce Chinese?" "The more trouble they have selling something, the more they advertize!" "Watching this program is a waste of time!" "Go ahead, make a fool of yourself, but quit striking a pose." "Now aren't we a pair of old fools with nothing better to do than stare at these stupid programs!" "I'll be damned if I watch TV again tomorrow!" The language became rougher and rougher.

The next day, the old question came up: what to do after dinner? News was still worth watching. After all, aren't we all interested in events at home and abroad? The couple actually felt obliged to the car accidents, break outs of war, airplane accidents, leaking oil tanks, assassinations of presidents, beaching of whales, poaching of elephants. . . . They felt obliged to the world for supplying TV with stimulating material, thankful to TV programs for offering them these attractions. They were also thankful not to be swallowed by a whale, killed by a bomb, or involved in an airplane crash.

Having watched the news, they decided to see what followed. At least there was the weather forecast. Having the TV on didn't interfere with doing other things. It is said that it's "trendy" to keep the TV on, keeping the volume low. Watch if you feel like it, ignore it if you don't.

But the couple couldn't bring themselves to do this. Once turned on, they had to watch. Why turn on the TV if not to watch? Could you imagine turning it on so as not to watch? There was always the possibility they'd hit upon a good program. Besides, at an unconscious level, they were calculating the financial costs: by keeping the TV on, the electricity meter was ticking away at over ten cents an hour. Besides, the machine itself was kept running. And this machine cost them their combined incomes for six months. Since both the electric meter and the machine were running, wouldn't it be a shame not to watch? Wouldn't it be adding waste to waste? Wouldn't it be too disrespectful to other people's labor—the combined labor of people at the electricity bureau, the generator plant, the technical personnel, the broadcaster, the producer and the cast of the TV station, as well as their own labor? Without their own labor, how could the TV set be where it was?

Better turn it off. But what to do next? Take a walk? They had already walked some distance going to work and coming home. Read? Tiring to the eyes and the mind. Listen to music? No fun without visuals. Visit friends or relatives? *They* would be watching TV. Turning it off lasts for only half an hour, since there is no better alternative. You are dissatisfied with TV. True, but maybe even more dissatisfied without TV. According to the evening papers, turning the machine on and off would hurt the kinescope and waste more electricity—even more than leaving the machine on. The more you try to save, the more you waste.

Might as well make do with what you have. Good thing there's something to watch. Besides, lounging lazily on the sofa and watching aimlessly has become a habit. And habits are hard to break. Thus, their comments cooled down. "It's not too bad after all! Not intolerable." "That T-shirt doesn't look bad at all. Next time you see one like it, you mustn't forget to buy one!" "How come we've never seen XX before? How come we haven't seen YY recently?" "Ha, this star is not above doing commercials!" "Foreign films? And what's so special about foreign films? They are second-rate, just like our own!"

Sometimes, the wife would make a bizarre comment,

leaving her husband completely baffled. For instance, after seeing episode after episode of a certain TV drama, the wife said, "Ha! It's so fake it looks real!" The husband was lost in admiration. What he appreciated was not the TV drama, but his wife's comment. What does it mean, "It's so fake it looks real"? The husband mulled it over for a long time without finding an answer. He was grateful for this TV drama, grateful to it for inspiring such an ingenious aphorism and setting him thinking. Otherwise, such a dull-witted person as himself would not qualify to be part of the thinking generation. On second thoughts, isn't the thinking generation itself so fake that it looks real? Might as well stick to the generation on screen.

In this fashion their affair with the TV proceeded from honeymoon to crisis to reconciliation. Thesis, antithesis, synthesis, Hegel, negation of the negative. All in all the couple's progression of TV-watching was normal, understandable, and actually quite commendable.

"Comparisons are the root of all evil." This saying should be collected in "Famous Sayings of the Famous." If this couple is not famous enough to be included in that prestigious collection, it might be used in an advertisement column or end up in the animated cartoons.

Coming down as we are now to a certain Day of a certain Month of a certain Year, it happened that the wife went to visit a classmate and together they watched TV for the evening. As soon as the wife returned home, discontent set in. The wife said, "It's really as the saying goes, 'You don't know a thing if you don't compare; and once you compare, you get a scare!'" She said, "Their TV is the real thing—so clear, so bright, so fine, so reliable, so accurate, so clean, so soft, so multifunctional, so luxurious! Better than going to the movies at the Majestic, the Dahua, the Paramount, the True Light, the Moon Palace, the deluxe section and even the super deluxe section of the Silver Star!" The wife said: "Compared with other people's TV, ours is not TV but a slide projector; not even a slide projector but a shivering, fuzzy, foggy, colorless, shapeless Aggravator!"

The husband kept his cool. Generally speaking, family rhythm is maintained by the wife keeping cool when the husband is worked up and the husband keeping cool when the wife is worked up; by the husband being at a loss if the wife is neither worked up nor cool, and the wife in hysterics if the husband is neither worked up nor cool . . . This is why harmony is never possible between husband and wife. And this is why husband and wife are forever inseparable. Anyway, this is how this couple maintains equilibrium in their relationship. Supposing on the contrary, the husband yells and the wife screams, supposing the husband's anger rises three degrees and the wife's caps it with four, and then the husband's fury shoots up seven degrees and the wife's matches it with ten . . . Then forget it, it would be the end of the relationship!

The cool husband asked, "What is the make of their TV? If ours is no good, let's save some more money and buy another one. It's not as if we were buying a house or land. Not as if. . . ."

The agitated wife said, "It's not a question of the brand. They said it's a matter of fine tuning. . . ."

"Then why don't you do some tuning," the husband said. The husband actually didn't believe in the power of tuning. The year before, he too had tried some fine tuning. Not only that, but he had installed several sets of "antenna systems." He had tried the indoor rabbit ears, the outdoor ring, the homemade outdoor kind made with the easy-to-pull Coca-Cola can, and the imported fishbone variety bought with Foreign Exchange Certificates. The husband said "You adjust it," but to himself he added, "I don't believe you can do it!" Usually, adjusting the TV was the job of the husband; the wife didn't interfere. Thus, the husband became sensitive; criticizing the TV was implicitly criticizing him. Praising other people's TV was tantamount to praising other people's husbands. "Huh," the husband snorted, a hint of a sneer in his voice, "I am not good enough. You take over."

The wife began her adjusting. First she tried the four antennas one by one. The trouble was, none of them was better than the others. The ring antenna didn't work as well as the rabbit ears, the-easy-to-pull can was not as good as the ring type, and the fishbone was less satisfactory than the easy-to-pull can. Might as well go back to the rabbit ears. But by then the rabbit ears didn't perform as well as the fishbone! Even so, she stuck to it. Extending it and shortening it, turning it first to the right and then to the left. The more she adjusted, the worse it got. After quite a while, she was grateful that the original image was restored. That's the best she could do.

"Is it better now?" the wife asked.

"No," answered the husband.

"Is it better now?" The wife made another try.

"No," said the husband.

"Is it better now?" the wife asked anxiously after trying again.

"Can't see much difference," the husband answered coolly.

The wife broke out in a sweat. She didn't look to her husband any more. She backed up and looked at the screen herself, saying with satisfaction, "It's much better," meaning, "I'm much better than you at this!"

The husband remained silent.

The wife asked, "Honestly, is it better?"

The husband must make a choice: if he wanted to act

130

according to courtesy, goodwill, friendship, love, duty, a sense of mission, good breeding, the minimum standards of civilization or the wish to preserve family harmony, he most certainly should have said, "I agree, much better!"

Yet it would not be according to his conscience. According to his conscience, he saw no improvement; perhaps it was even worse.

Why is it that he could not see any improvement however much he stared at the screen? Yet his wife kept insisting that it was better. Now why did he want to take issue with his wife? Was he deliberately making trouble? Was he provoking his wife? Was he out of love with his wife? Was this an emotional crisis? Was there someone else? Was he an unfaithful husband? Did he intend to abandon his wife for another woman, like a modern Chen Shimei? Was he in a bad mood? Losing his mental balance? Unfairly treated at work? Suffering from eye trouble? Was he just being perverse? Was he being uncooperative? Was he a spoil sport? Had he taken some wrong medicine? Was he undergoing puberty? Menopause? And, oh, there's Freud, should he check into a mental hospital?

Why bother? He was neither so bad nor so morbid. Relax and everything will be fine. It was hard to be clever, but harder to be a fool. And even harder to transfer from the one to the other. Concede a point, retreat a step, anything for peace and quiet. Arguing back and forth over trifles gets you nowhere. What's wrong with submitting? That takes real skill.

"All right," he managed to say without wincing.

"Really better?" This time the wife showed humility, sincerely asking for her husband's opinion.

"Really better," he said casually.

"Are you speaking the truth?" The wife was suspicious.

"I . . ." the husband was at a loss for words. So that's it, no matter what he said, he couldn't get it right. What should he do? He struggled with himself.

"Don't humor me! I spent so much time adjusting it, is it really better? You must tell the truth. Why am I doing this? I never watch sports competitions myself . . ."

"Too late for sports programs now," the husband said dejectedly. On the screen, the Argentine umpire was blowing the whistle, Milan versus Belgium: 0-0.

"Please speak the plain truth! Did I make any improvement? If not, I'll do some more adjusting. You have missed a sports program today. Let's make it worth the sacrifice. You can't imagine how good the reception can be once we fix it, how wonderful the image . . ."

"I've said it over and over again—good, good, good! I'm 100 percent truthful, not one false word. Your adjustment was good." The husband was actually about to say, "No better." The "n" sound almost escaped from his lips. But when the wife said that she would do some more adjusting, he decided to admit it was "Better!" And he was determined never to go back on his word, never to overturn the verdict! Never.

"Huh." The wife let out a deep breath. "See how sharp the image is! In the past year, we've never had it so clear. It is excellent, excellent!" The husband felt forlorn. The game was over, the screen was showing advertisement for cosmetics. Of course the pictures in the advertisement were just as clear as the ones from a fool's touch-on camera, certainly better than the live broadcast from an outdoor stadium. How could you say this was the result of adjusting? But what could he do? Argue? With whom? With his wife? Argue with his dear wife? To challenge the good results of her adjusting? Who would benefit by his challenging his wife's accomplishment? But who would benefit if he ac-

132

knowledged his wife's accomplishment? What did he expect by denying his wife's accomplishment? Change to another antenna? Change the TV, or change a wife? Did he deserve something like that? Could he do it, considering the expense and energy required? The options being so clear, why hesitate?

Thus, the husband's helpless bitter smile changed to a heartfelt sweet smile. He even went over and stroked his wife's hair.

"Heh? How come it's bad again?" The wife came back from the bathroom to find the screen looking worse. The husband also found the picture less sharp than before.

"It's possibly the station's problem," the husband said. Seeing his wife's gloomy face, he added, "It might also be a question of voltage." Since the face was still gloomy, he went on, "There may be some kind of interference . . . something about the weather."

"Impossible," said the wife, "don't try to fool me. You think I don't understand. Our machine has a voltage stablizer, automatically adjusting to changing pressure." The wife went outdoors to take a look. "Besides, there is not even a cloud in the sky. As to TV parts, these are imported. No problem about quality, therefore no interference." One by one, the wife marshalled her rebuttals to each of her husband's anticipated arguments. Finally, the wife pointed a finger at her husband's nose and said, "I know. You moved the antenna."

"I didn't move it."

"Yes, you did."

"I didn't."

"You did."

"I didn't."

"You did! You must have done it!" the wife shouted.

"It's. . . . possible that I. . . . did move it." The husband recalled the famous sayings of sages, and familiar quotations from commercials. He felt he had achieved a new understanding.

The wife let out a groan and gradually quieted down, since the husband has admitted his guilt. An admission was an admission, even if it had been a case of wrecking the kinescope. Then the wife went back to experimenting with the antenna, changing its length, direction, and angle. She renewed her questions one by one, still dissatisfied. Suddenly she announced, "Should the outdoor antennas be changed?"

The wife painstakingly climbed to the rooftop to adjust the outdoor antenna—both the imported one bought with Foreign Exchange Certificates and the native, handmade one. The husband was moved to make several trips to the rooftop too. This went on until every channel announced "Thank you" and "Goodbye."

Adjusting continued the following day, first the antenna, then fine tuning. Problems abounded. One touch and the picture went bad, even the color disappeared, leaving the screen all black or all white. All kinds of strange dots and lines showed up on screen. Voices became hoarse, eventually fading away. These kinds of trouble would crop up without a warning. But that was not the worst. If that was the only trouble, all you needed to do was to reverse the procedure to recover the original. The worst was after exhausting yourself turning fifteen degrees to the left and twenty-five degrees to the right, then ten degrees to the left and eight degrees to the right, then pulling out the antenna three millimeters and then pushing it back two millimeters . . . Just when you thought you'd fixed it, you are left completely at a loss. You can't even tell whether it's better or worse. If you can't see any improvement, nor any change for the worse, then according to logic there had been no change. Yet you suspect change. That is to say, not only are you unable to decide whether things got better or worse, you can't even tell if there had been any change at all.

Thus the wife continually asked her husband for his opinion. She depended on his views as her sole point of reference. The husband thus continued to say, "Good" "Good" "Good." When she pulled the antenna longer, he said, "Good." When she shortened it, he also said, "Good."

"Is it better longer or shorter?" The wife became agitated.

"Both are good," said the husband.

"How is it possible that both are good?" The wife's temper rose.

He was indignant. "Then both are not good."

When the husband's response was positive, the wife became angry. When the husband's response was negative, the wife became suspicious.

This kind of adjusting and tuning not only interfered with their TV viewing, it also created a barrier between them. Sincerity merely led to conflict, while pretense further widened the gap. They were trapped in a vicious circle; they descended into an abyss.

"Why don't you speak the truth? Why are you always so evasive, dodging questions all the time? What do you really think of me? Between us, is there still the kind of love that is intense, sincere, selfless, intoxicating, and beautiful?" The wife tearfully brought up this grave issue. She went on to ask, "Whom have you fallen in love with?"

"But . . . but . . ." the husband felt sad, apologetic, almost as if the question was pointless. It was dreadful. People say that husband and wife can hug or fight each other, can sing love songs or fling abuses at each other, or get mad at each other. In short, anything goes except ending up with a feeling of pointlessness.

For this reason, the husband offered his own explanation of the situation. The quality of the TV reception was dependent on many factors—for instance, the quality of the transmission, which in turn was dependent on technology, software, materials, machinery, and hardware. Then it could be an operational problem, or a matter of adjustment. It could also be traced back to quality of parts, assembly, and the weather. Moreover, one should not expect the same quality for different kinds of screen images. For example, how could you compare a night scene of safebreaking with a bright summer beach scene with foreign women in bikinis? Could both look equally clear, bright, and enchanting? Even if you adjusted the wretched thing to death, you could not achieve the same quality.

The husband said, "Don't be too particular. Don't ask for perfection. If the water is too clear, there won't be any fish; if you scrutinize people too closely, no one will stay by you. There is no pure gold; there is no perfect man. The state of TV perfection is fleeting, dependent on many factors: weather, interference, energy . . . It needs constant adjusting to maintain. But on the other hand, if you go on adjusting, you might as well not watch."

The wife had nothing to say. What the wife hated most was her husband's systems of logic. For example, if the wife wanted to eat cold flavored tofu and the husband preferred sautéed, he would marshall all sorts of arguments. On the other hand, if he wanted his tofu cold and she chose to have it sautéed, again logic, logic, logic. Oppressive logic. Maddening logic. Why couldn't he just say he wanted sautéed tofu, or whatever it was? Why drag in logic? Logic, like patriarchy, state power, church rule, or the concept of chastity, they're all shackles for women's liberation. Signs of male chauvinism. A rope tied around women. Male logic was like a big, fat guy taking up all the space and squeezing the tiny goddess of love right out of the room.

The wife had nothing more to say. Silently she shed tears. From then on, when watching TV, no matter how terrible the screen image, she would sit absolutely motionless. All she could do was to shed a few tears from time to time. Eventually, even her tears dried up.

The husband, on the other hand, was restless. His hands just itched to do something about the TV. The thought that it was his wife who had ruined the quality of the reception dogged him like a ghost. The idea that he could make improvements tempted him like the female snake spirit. He began to adjust the antennas, to fine tune, to fiddle with all the knobs and devices. First he made small changes, then medium ones, then major ones. He was like a man possessed.

"Is it better?" the husband asked.

"No," the wife answered.

"Is it better?" the husband asked again.

"No," the wife answered.

"Is it better now?" The husband's voice was anxious.

"Can't see any change," the wife answered coolly.

The husband was sweating. He gave up faith in her. He stepped back to take a look himself.

A hint of a smile crossed the wife's face. The situation was reversed: whoever meddles bears the anxiety, the bystander is the judge. Really interesting.

The two of them almost ended in divorce over the TV. The two of them became inseparable over the fine tuning. The process furthermore revealed to both their own stupidity, prejudice, conceit, and the fact that they were both completely out of touch with reality. The same process also led them to compromise, mutual consideration, and support. Above all, tuning and adjusting the TV turned out to be more fun than watching. They were now no longer upset by any TV programs, no matter how inferior.

After one last ruthless adjustment, the husband applied a soldering iron to all the knobs on the machine. He effectively finished off the set.

Coincidentally, the wife won the raffle and went and bought a completely automatic, super-model TV set. Aside from choosing a channel, the viewer didn't need to lift a finger.

"Isn't this a fool's touch-on TV set?" The husband was not impressed. "So, besides a fool's camera, we have a fool's TV. Who knows when there will be a fool's cooking pot, a fool's wine maker, a fool's drawing gadget—everything will be self-adjusted to a uniform, optimum standard," the husband said sarcastically.

The wife paid no attention to him. She was extremely satisfied with the images on the fool's TV and its computerized, automatic tuning devices.

Life would be perfect if only there could be a fool of a husband. She said to herself, "Fools are the best."

"After all, we are a fortunate couple," the husband said. He kissed his wife's shoulder and savored the true meaning of happiness.

In a moment of relative wakefulness he was struck by how unusually precious that blanket was. The thought stabbed at his heart. The blanket was like a colored cloud at twilight after rain; how could anyone bear to part with it? By comparison, the recent additions to their bedroom had been excessive, even burdensome. The Western-style mattress, the brocade bedspread, the floss quilt, the down quilt, the dog-skin cotton-padded mattress that had no use once they had the Western-style mattress, the camel-hair mattress, . . . and the endless supply of towels used for covering pillows. The spilt-bamboo mats they used for sleeping during hot summers had turned green with mold because they hadn't washed them in timely fashion. They bought new ones from Guangdong, yet hadn't seen fit to throw away the old ones. Just the blankets they had accumulated were now beyond counting: the Shanghai and the Tianjin blankets, the Lahore-style and the regular ones, the imports from Pakistan and the ones they brought back from Australia, the polyester blends and the all-wool blankets. . . . But that purple woolen blanket topped them all. It was burning, and gradually receding into darkness.

After he woke up he felt unclear about all this. Had there ever been such a blanket? Maybe not. Could they perchance have sold it—during a move, or at the beginning of the Red Guard campaign, or when policies reverted and they were reassigned housing, or when a peddler may have visited their door? Or had it been stolen? Hadn't they been burglarized once, back around 1976 or 1977? They had filed a police report. . . .

He asked his wife, "Did we ever own a purple woolen blanket?"

His wife nodded vaguely. She had suffered a stroke that had impaired her walking and left her with a partial speech impediment. She spent all day just smiling at televi-

Chamber Music I and II

I. The Twilight Cloud

That night Old Zhang (or should we say Respected Zhang the Elder?) was slumbering along when he recalled (or dreamed, maybe?) that his wife owned a purple woolen blanket. Yes, he thought—it was the one they had bought shortly after they were married. In those days the classiest, most exquisite item in their new apartment had been that soft, warm, thick, splendidly colored blanket. All the other neighborhood families, whose status was about the same as theirs, and who were also setting up new households, opted for motley gray-and-white cotton blankets with two dyed red stripes showing through. These cotton blankets always gave you the feeling they might snap in half when folded, because the folds exposed the "burlap" nature of their basic weave.

Struggling to wake up, but still in limbo between wakefulness and sleep, Old Zhang was taken with anxiety about the whereabouts of that woolen blanket. How peculiar! For many years—ten years, or perhaps eight, or anyway, at least five, but certainly no fewer than three—they had forgotten about that blanket and neglected to use it. By now they had not even *seen* the purple woolen blanket for many years—ten, it seemed.

sion broadcasts or videotapes; it mattered not whether these were athletic contests, lectures in foreign languages, TV dramas, ads for insect repellents, or reports on currency exchange rates. In the past, he mused, she could even play the accordion!

He turned the place upside down. Ruefully he noted that he had probably used up as much of his limited life span searching for things as he had spent being an inspector. Regaining his equanimity, he reflected that searching for things and being an inspector are both important components of life. There wasn't any blanket—not the one he remembered or had imagined; there were only the other blankets that had been purchased later on and that he didn't really need. But he did discover two and a half pairs of socks that had been worn who knows how long ago and hadn't been washed. It was good, he thought, that they had not yet decomposed into mustard gas.

He asked his ex-accordionist wife, who used to play "Long Flows the Volga," if they had indeed bought a purple woolen blanket in the year they were married. "Brightly colored—soft, thick, warm . . . ?" he reminded her.

His wife vaguely shook her head, smiling, tears welling in her eyes. She turned to look at the television screen, where an exquisitely beautiful woman was falling from the sky. Then she mumbled, "In the mornings . . . very expensive . . . they're for sale." A long time later she was still telling herself, "They're—for—sale."

Later, Respected Zhang the Elder was diverted to other things. He had an argument with his children, and when the argument was over he'd forgotten about the blanket. Yet there were a few times during the ensuing year—either when he was trying to sleep but couldn't or when he was trying to wake up but couldn't—that the thought of that blanket hit him again with special urgency. In those moments he felt sure that there had indeed been a blanket, and that its loss was indeed extremely regrettable. Not having looked for the blanket in a timely manner was, moreover, his own unforgivable fault. He even felt that to have treated the blanket in such a cold, uncaring, and inhumane manner might be a frightening sign of something. His emotions, his mental powers, and his mind itself became exhausted to the point of dysfunction.

Some time later—not a short time, but not a long one either—his wife died.

After the funeral he went home, but found he could no longer recognize the place. He doubted even whether he'd actually lived there for five years. A curtain of brown oil spots covered the kitchen wall. A screw had fallen from the doorknob of the bedroom door; no kind of twist could turn the knob, yet the door opened anyway. A mild breeze would cause air to seep through the window frames, making a sound like the sigh of a beast under a butcher's knife. There were many other things that should have been attended to long ago; how could it be that he hadn't noticed?

When he couldn't sleep at night he became ever more clearly aware of that blanket, whose color only seemed to grow more elegant with time, whose soft texture he could feel, whose warmth and weight were his when he imagined pulling it over himself. Then the blanket would float away. He would follow it, and in its company revisit the houses they had once lived in. He saw a long, single-story, narrow building divided into apartments, one of which had been theirs. The outside was graced by evergreens, canna, and plantain lilies; a purple butterfly perched on one of the blossoms. The inside was both fresh and warm. He could swim around in the apartment like a little fish, his body extending far, far as he swam. He could bend in any way, or move in circles. He adored this apartment. His wicker carrying case seemed still to be there, along with his little bookshelf, his washbasin, and a desk lamp he himself had made. There was a bed plank that had belonged to him. When he joined the communist movement and left home to live in one of the organization's dormitories, he had brought three such planks and two wooden benches with him. The planks didn't quite fit together snugly, but he had had many nights of wonderful sleep on them nonetheless. Later he had been transferred to another unit, and then to another city, and some time after that had come back to where he started. But he had not taken the planks with him on this circle route, and they had been converted from private to public property—different from nowadays, when public property is converted to private. Now three planks and two long benches ought to be waiting inside that house for him to use or to carry away. There should also be a photograph in the house—his wedding photo, showing him with his lips smeared bright red and his wife's eyes smeared brownish green like a cat's. That photo, ever youthful, always hung there; when a breeze rustled the window curtain, the him in the photo would smile. The corners of that mouth would dance impishly; but the eyes of his wife seemed about to shed tears.

He woke up, heaving a sigh that shook the house. Suddenly an inspiration came. He had—without a doubt—stuck that purple blanket deep into the closet that was above the door. The closet was beyond his reach, so he found two chairs, stacked one atop the other, and then, risking a broken leg or even a broken back, climbed up to look. He found no blanket, but only stirred up a lot of pale brown dust, which in turn sent him into a fit of coughing. He couldn't understand why the dust was pale brown. He also found some ragged pieces of paper bearing some "poetry" he had written a few decades ago. Poetry?!

After a few days, old friends began advising him that

he should pull his life back together. Some told him how important it would be, from a health standpoint, to find another missus. They said people with spouses live on the average 15 to 20 percent longer than lonely widowers do. Others spoke of the special enchantment of "romance in the golden years." He thought the term "romance in the golden years" sounded real nice. It made him think of rosy twilight clouds, and he burned.

He didn't say yes, but he didn't say no either. And so it happened, with the help of some friends who cared deeply for him, that he began to meet some women. One of these ladies, whose hair was dyed jet black, wore a tight-fitting coat made of coarse, grayish-white fabric. From the back she looked quite like a young girl, and her speech carried an appealing dash of Shanghai accent. But, unfortunately, he found something not quite right about that accent—as well as about her complexion and the style of her eyeglasses. There was also something vaguely awkward about the size and arrangement of her teeth. She wasn't for him.

Yet, in the end, they did have some contact. They spent one summer evening together at a teahouse in the park, where they ordered a pot of Dragon Well tea, chatted as they cracked and ate melon seeds, and recounted for each other their various comings and goings over the better part of a lifetime.

When he went home afterward he felt extremely clearheaded. Clearheaded but exhausted. Other than to lie on his bed clearheadedly, he couldn't, and didn't want to, do anything else. The weather seemed sweltering, making him loath to cover himself with his quilt; but he wasn't accustomed to leaving it off either. After a while he sat up—for no real reason—and inadvertently bumped the bedding on his wife's bed. Suddenly, under the mattress, he noticed a purple blanket.

Entirely contrary to what he had imagined, the blanket now barely engaged his feelings or his interest. It was no twilight cloud. It bore no poetic feeling. The old thing had no life or particular charm; moreover it had begun to turn a pale brown—the color of that dust in the closet above his door. It wasn't necessarily the same blanket.

After that, however, he never had tea again with that lady who looked from the back like a young girl but actually had a lot of years to her credit. He offered the excuse that he wanted to go live with his children for a while. He had to leave the city, and might not even come back at New Year's.

"Sorry."

He was going to add, "I feel so embarrassed," but the words didn't come out. He somehow felt that phrases like this had been brought into the language by Chinese from Taiwan or America—by what you might call "bourgeois" types. Should he imitate their speaking styles? He was, don't forget, pretty old.

II. Poetic Feeling

When Professor Liu turned fifty-nine he suddenly became a stutterer. In his youth he had been famous for his sprightly tongue and flowing eloquence. The quality of his voice had been pleasing too. People who heard him speak a few sentences often would ask if he had taken voice lessons. But now, stuttering, stammering, and hoarse, he seemed utterly helpless.

It began to dawn on him that talk is the most important thing in life. Everything is either expressed by or decided by talk. Victory and defeat, praise and punishment, the sublime and the vile, love and hate, wealth and poverty, the great and the petty, intelligence and stupidity, truth and falsehood—all these are maintained by, distinguished through, formed of, and undermined by talk. Let's face it, life *is* talk. And here he was, still several years from retirement, and talk had already become an obstacle. My god.

He went to quite a few hospitals, herbal clinics, and medical schools in search of a cure. Practitioners of every approach exhausted all their diagnostic tools—checking inside and out, upside and down, stripping him to his elemental parts and putting him back together again—but found nothing wrong.

He had no alternative but to seek help within his own intuition and imagination. In the still of night he would attune himself to the sun and moon, the starry firmament, and the wind and dew. In probing his deepest self, he hoped for an answer. Over many years, at many forks and passes in life, whenever he had felt the burden of worry over what to do, his last and strongest resort had always been this kind of deep self-interrogation and the scrupulous heed to the inner voice. Experience had shown that the judgments and choices that resulted were, on the whole, not bad.

By this route he gained sudden enlightenment. The problem was his pillow.

For several decades he had used the pillow that his parents had given him as a boy. The pillow itself was made of village-spun cloth that had been sewn into a bag and stuffed with buckwheat husks. When he slept he sometimes spread a towel or piece of linen on top. Sometimes he put nothing on top. He didn't know the history of the pillow, but was sure it had seen more of the world than he had. The village-spun cloth was so sturdy! Never mind how coarse and uneven it might be, or how full of ridges, knots, and burrs. After years of use the cloth on his pillow, and even the buckwheat husks inside, had absorbed his perspiration and the oil from his hair until now it emitted a distinctive odor, which somewhat resembled chocolate.

His wife had advised him long ago to change pillows. She went to stores and came back with every manner of alternative: pillows stuffed with down, with kapok, with cattail wool, with tea leaves; rectangular pillows and square pillows; and pillowcases of every color and design. He declined everything on the grounds that he was used to the old pillow and that it was still pretty good. His son ridiculed him by saying that the pillow should long ago have been sent to a museum. It should, said the son, count as a treasure of "family essence," just as kung fu and the martial arts are treasures of China's "national essence." His daughter held her nose as she blamed his pillow for polluting the air—which, she said, had been none too clean to start with. He himself began to feel that the ancient pillow didn't actually fit very well with the other furnishings in the bedroom and apartment that they had renovated several times. Finally, six months ago, he threw the old pillow away.

Looking back, he now realized that it was just one month after switching to a new pillow that he developed his slight stutter. It was after two months that the minor hoarseness set in. Things got steadily worse from then on, until now his voice and speech just weren't what they should be. He asked his wife and children, and the children's governess, where the old pillow had gone. If it was still around, where was it? Could it be washed and patched for reuse? If it was not still around, who threw it away? When? Where? Strangely, the answer was always, "I don't know," and the manner of the answer's delivery seemed designed to make him believe that the pillow simply did not exist—or that, if it had indeed continued existing for a while, it had later disappeared on its own.

He pursued the matter, intensely and often, with his family and the governess. Eventually this triggered a backlash. "It's *your* pillow, and your business. If anybody lost it, you did. If somebody threw it away, you're that person."

It was true. There was nothing he could say.

He decided to pay a visit to his home village. One after another, officials in the township, district, and county stepped forth to banquet him on wheatcakes, stewed pork, fresh fish, and deep-fried quail. These people were concentrating on things like chemical fertilizers, plastics, lumber, cement, and glass, as well as on the barter of gifts that made all this business possible. When he raised the topic of his pillow, his village friends told him that these days everybody, even the peasants, use pillows that are shipped in from places like Beijing, Shanghai, Tianjin, and Suzhou. The pillows are "soft and squishy, with embroidered flowers," they said.

"What about the ones made with buckwheat chaff?"

"We haven't planted buckwheat in years," explained a village official. "It doesn't produce very much, and it's hard to digest. . . . We've got chemical fertilizer now, and irrigation—we can't exactly waste fertilizer and irrigation on something like buckwheat."

He knew that buckwheat was grown only in the marginal lands of remote or mountainous areas. But he would not accept that it is hard to digest. And besides, he was not asking for a bowl of buckwheat noodles.

"All I need is some buckwheat husks," he said.

"If we have no buckwheat how can we give you buckwheat husks?" The local official did, of course, have a point here.

After wandering several miles through the neighboring villages, he finally did find some buckwheat husks. But he couldn't find any homespun cloth. He asked everywhere, but there wasn't any. All he could find were a few dilapidated peasant looms. As he fondled a shuttle on one of the looms, he thought of the cliché, "The days pass like arrows, the months like flying shuttles."

He returned to the city, smoldering in frustration. His stuttering and hoarseness grew even worse. Every syllable was a chore. He gradually became reluctant to talk at all. Illness can change a person's nature, even his worldview. He began to think. Yes, talk was the root of everything; but not talking gave rise to another everything that was even more valuable. He kept on thinking.

His quest for buckwheat husks and village-spun cloth caused him to reminisce. Every night scenes of his youth came to him in dreams. He saw his grandmother spinning yarn; the sound of the spinning wheel broke his heart. He saw, inside his boyhood home, the two big vases that held feather dusters; sun shining on the chicken feathers produced a shimmering iridescence. He saw himself swimming with his boyhood buddies in summertime; diving into the water, they competed to see who could stay under the longest and swim the farthest before emerging. He also saw a big, black dog that kept licking his face with its wet tongue, until he feared it might take a bite of him. But the fear was mixed with sweetness and delight. The gaze of that dog was so deep, steady, and mature—like that of a philosopher who sees into your soul. . . . He also saw a cheerful sparrow, chirping.

What the heck, he thought—I'll just basically give up on talk and instead write down all of my recollections, musings, feelings, and dreams. His wife pronounced him ill and wanted to send him to the hospital, but his children said he had become a poet, and a good one at that. Without asking his permission, the children sent his writings off to some high-circulation literary periodicals in Beijing. His poems were published and he became an overnight success. On the brink of retirement, he had become the new flowering in Chinese poetry. All those poets and critics who had flowered long ago now toasted him, feted him, and gave him prizes. His name found its way into a literary encyclopedia. For this he sent 250 Chinese dollars to the encyclopedia's editors.

A few years later, it was said, these literary magazines came in for criticism. His poems were declared to be not good. They contained unhealthy sentiments; they "toyed" with literature; they sprang from Western influences. They were like taking drawstrings that Americans had grown bored with and wrapping them around one's neck like a muffler. . . .

An elderly relative—who, if you reckon the family tree properly, was in his grandmother's generation—came from the countryside to visit him. The old man advised against writing any more poetry. Gambling, grave-robbing, whoring, looting, severing telephone lines, and killing pandas were all better than writing poetry. The man also brought him a pillow made from village-spun cloth and buckwheat husks. He said times had changed again. Native products were back on the upswing—the more primitive and native, the better. Only through primitive and native things could China reach out to the world, win prizes and earn foreign currency. This is why their village had established a Traditional Pillow Processing Plant and had named a physically handicapped villager to be its head. In its first year the plant earned sixty thousand Chinese dollars.

And so he once again could sleep on a buckwheat-chaff pillow. He also regularly took Chinese herbal medicine. The ingredients of this medicine were mulberry leaves, silkworm skins, cicada shells, scorpion tails, safflower, root of milk vetch, blood ginseng, creat, amber, cinnabar, and Asian plantain, mixed together with the urine of boys three years old or younger. The boys' urine, a catalytic agent, was said to be especially efficacious in dissipating excessive body heat. According to the most experienced and authoritative people, if he took two hundred doses of this medicine, and wrote no poetry while under treatment, and slept every night on his buckwheat-chaff pillow, he would unquestionably see results. He was certain to make a full recovery and to regain his former eloquence. He could look forward to scaling new heights in his senior years, to a future without limit, and so on.

"To Alice"

One morning, hardly do I find time for my new novella when the newly installed musical doorbell rings. It has the tune of "To Alice," but none of the pitches is right, sounding like the feeble yet hysterical moanings of an old woman who has not eaten for three days. I hurry to open the door, and there stands a smiling, graceful young man with long hair.

"Are you writing novels?"

"Well . . ."

"How come the novels you write can get published and win awards? Please be honest with me, if I had written those novels of yours with my name on them, would they get published?"

"Well, it . . . it . . . for instance, in the past, when I observed others' poor handwriting . . ."

"Don't you lecture me, please. You are neither Wang Xizhi nor Hui Su or me either, but I like writing stories. I have inspiration; I'm molding language. You're playing with it! An editor once said this. But what is this 'playing with'? Long Ping has several spikes and suddenly sneaks in with a drop shot. Is she 'playing with' the ball? Tell me, come on . . ."

"Er, er . . ."

"Aren't there some like you, seemingly to have created something new. In fact you're blocking our way. Step aside, please, leave us some paper to print our stuff . . ."

"However, I see no conflict . . ."

"Then have a look at this novice piece of mine. Let's first agree not to get angry. If you can't get used to it, just treat it like I haven't written it at all, then everything will be okay. One sells to those who appreciate . . ."

He did not write much so I finished reading pretty fast. Full of shitty nonsense, but not without satire; there is at least something in his ability to use stream of consciousness. Probably a sense of humor, though not of a high order. I now know what comments I have for him, but he is nowhere to be found. He has quietly left while I am reading his "Green Sun." I walk to the door of the compound, looking left and right. Quite a few young men with long hair are passing, either walking or riding bikes, but not him. I summon my courage and plan to publish this "piece of writing," hoping its writer will soon contact me. If he doesn't within the deadline of three months, I will donate the contribution fee to the Xuanwu Gate Nursery on his behalf.

P.S. After he comes and leaves, my doorbell breaks down. I have no idea if he knows why.

Green Sun

I wake up all my family at midnight, saying look isn't there a green sun in the sky because our quartz wall clock has won a Nobel Prize. Wife says I am kidding there is no sun says fry me two balloons to stop dysentery and increase potency. Son pushes me away and goes on sleeping declaring if he cannot go abroad he will marry that older girl who plays Erhu. Father mumbles sky used to have nine suns then flew away far and wide after growing up and never returned. Daughter says she wants to buy a Toyota she wants to enroll in corre-spondence-night-TV universities improving résumé getting diplomas and full tuition refund from her employer nearly a thousand yuan. Wife says if you don't eat apples they will rot more and probably price will increase.

I carry a shovel on my shoulder and plant trees near the sign of a bus station. I am fantasizing a helicopter may land before the tree bears mushroom clouds, dig out a toad that can speak write ingratiate. Not only can the toad croak but also bark neigh bellow crow, speak altogether four five foreign languages not knowing after coming back what for-eign country he got his diploma in. I ask toad why it doesn't wear toady sunglasses it says afraid of being aloof bad im-pression among people. I suddenly realize why there is no longer hope for my promotion fame hitting lottery. Bus comes but with no wheels, passengers all dig into their bags to give it some Ping-Pong balls mothballs black dates small bells huge baked cakes as wheels. Driver refuses to drive conductor refuses to sell tickets so everyone elects me in a democratic process to push it. I push it so fast that the Na-tional Athletics Commission selects me as coach of long me-dium short distance runners. I resign one month later to write stories and attend writers meetings in hell and stay in hotels because leadership doesn't give me free Western suit desk lamp sofa electric mosquito repeller art diary sheepskin jacket.

Hotel manager woos me in private, offers me sips of canned liquid gas, asks if I'm willing to be honorary chair of board of directors of Beauty Gruel, Inc., saying Beauty Gruel has already obtained a patent from Atlantic Trans-International Corp. and enjoys a special waive of income tax for fifteen days, emphasizing Beauty Gruel has vitamin U, V, W, XYZ as well as 2,437 kinds of organic compounds and in-organic salts. It has won Best Quality Cup after government tests and after taking it single-fold eyelids become twofold and twofold become fourfold plus legs grow forty centimeters longer. I ask if he has official written approval if approval has been circled if circle is round. He replies he's learned technique to draw circles with computerized compasses. I feel this manager's IQ is too low too mundane so suggest he go have gastrocopy at Sichuan Restaurant amputation at Editorial Department of People's Literature turn himself in at Editorial Department of Literature on Legality. He grows angry saying I'm too conservative with no sense for changing times has already lagged behind trends why not go to Shaolin Temple in Wudang Mountain to be a novice monk under Huo Yuanjia.

I go to see my first teacher whose name I've already forgotten only remember he is president chair speaker committee member member of standing council director office worker clerk probationer intern of the Shannan Hedong Research Institute. He has a bunch of larks busy debating and chirping along ever so cordially. They are exploring which is more important to eat millet or drink water. If ever millet is more important why the hell we need water if water is more crucial why the hell we need millet. If both are important which is to say none is important and this is unacceptable. Then if we say neither is crucial which is in fact to say both are important then why a lark has only one beak instead of two. My teacher very interestingly showers over them some insecticide Lysol health drug. From this symbol we come to realize how really crucial Halley's Comet is then say goodbye in English.

I feel sad painful stream of consciousness information feedback no way out night's eye and sound sleep. I sing Picasso late Impressionist school's precious timepiece Sony Toshiba that I cherish in my heart. I go to banquet hall feastfuls of wine meat and go find my second teacher who is living Tao Yuanming of contemporary time a scholar aloof alone cold as crescent moon hidden in sacred mountains fame enduring a thousand ages. I end up with taking subway to ruins of Yuanmingyuan Palace and chance meeting an Australian kangaroo I haven't seen for over a hundred years. A brown bear is serenading oh my flowery kerchief my little white poplar my chive fillings corn meal dough I'm most loyal to you. A cock roars with laughter a hen rises to graceful dance a drunk bear breaks to tears demanding a medal at an official ceremony. Out of a certain habit I go to shake its hand exchange greetings calling it brother then it says it wants to eat a human paw, to be a housemaid a kindergarten nanny. My second teacher rushes to explain it looks crude but really subtle and as kindhearted as Zhangfei's aunt. I give it a piece of pickle from Mars.

Then I go to see my elder brother who has long since become well known through stamp albums for good temper and no record of murders poisonings explosions. Every time he sees me he takes off hat bows 375 degrees and enthusiastically hugs heels of my yellow leather shoes. He publishes writings on the surface of sea eulogizing me as surpassing the ballerina Ulanovyava and offers to be my barber and a nine-wave perm. As I enter the door I hear him shouting it doesn't matter if he is my younger brother or not, I will not have crow noodles with fried bean sauce when it got to be sour stuffed dumplings! Even Lu Xun not to say my younger brother has to apply for residence write study reports look right and left while crossing streets. What's so special is my brother has he been to ant hive hitching eggs huge migration? I know he's again serving wine and feasts to Centaur Brand scotch gin with fingers that slice and preserve me. His individual character is to say things cheap shake hands cheap buy stuff cheap get sons cheap. In recent years he moves into phoenix nest but lacks egg yoke cholesterol steel frame. I turn back to leave he grabs me gives me steamed bread with sweet bean stuffing sings me a song "When Will You Come Back to Me" I ask to only take Weishuping yeast.

I find weather still okay world bustling with noise and excitement quality of ice cream better than Hong Kong even stones dance gracefully. I'm determined to join a spaceship trip to Mercury Saturn Star of Yin-Yang Eight Diagrams to attend an international academic conference. I will bring back a rebellious mini machine computer that can cry laugh beat one up kiss me kill me feed me oxygen and glycerine nitrate. I will make people be kind to and love one another and eat spicy pork cubes with braised lentil after it's done. I will make people extra sober after drinking my wine instead of getting drunk, after drinking my human-nature liquor they will be able to write poetry recite periodic table of elements, to comprehend speak write mother tongue son tongue daughter tongue son-in-law tongue of every country of United Nations. I will open a publishing house to specifically publish new songs of poets who are sobbing because they can't get their own poem collections published, the sale will surpass birthday cakes and Yamaha motorbikes, anyone who can write poetry will get for free five bat-styled shirts a suit for spring and fall and abstract Chinese little leaf box root sculptures. I will pull out teeth for give face-lifting to biased and testy cranes and dig out their enchanting smiles. I will distribute among middle elementary school teachers and shop assistants dragonfly tickets to tour Paris plus life insurance. I will establish a correspondence education center where Monkey King teaches how to grow kiwi fruit wine full of youthful potency capable of seventy-two metamorphoses. I will open garden cafeteria music saloon fancy restaurant requiring no written guarantee for customers. I will turn all laws into tiny boats street lamps into baked-cake-sugar-coated-haws sandwich. . . . But I don't know what'll become of this piece of writing, I sotto voce "To Alice."

Thrilling

The hero of this story, let's call him Xiang Ming, or Xiang Ning, or Xiang Ping, or Xiang Qing, or Xiang Ring, or Xiang Sing, or Xiang Ting, or Xiang Ving, and on and on ad infinitum. Three days ago, that is, five days ago a year ago two months later, he I mean she and it is afflicted with a cervical vertebra problem which means spine problem dental carries dysentery vitiligo breast cancer as well a clean bill of health and assurance of longevity.

Struck suddenly by a reeling dizziness on the forty-first of November, i.e., the eleventh and twelfth of the fourteenth month, hence takes X-ray B ultra-sound electroencephalogram cerebral angiography for final diagnosis. Couldn't get registration at hospital couldn't find personal connections therefore does not see doctor therefore forgets dizziness plays ball swims drinks gives speeches watches TV series in a word nothing wrong at all with cervical vertebra or in other words never had cervical vertebra in the first place. Relatives friends adversaries all rushed to assure him no one said a word you are so young you are so old you are hale and hearty you are on your last legs how can you be ill how come you're still alive and kicking! Talking thus makes him her it laugh out loud, howl with grief grunt groan mum's the word.

So takes super-luxury sedan and races on the freeway. After lots of trouble grabs a taxi, both eyes fixed on the meter, nagged by fears of being overcharged. Crossing newly reaped fields with stubble exposed and furrows unleveled, perched on an ox cart, buttocks jolted, really hurt. Passing through the bleak Gobi on a horse or better on a camel, now and then strange flora gives you the shivers. Seems like as far as a pair of feet is concerned, sandy desert or sandy beach it makes no difference. Airplane takes off, airline hostess brings juice with ice cubes and headsets for listening to dialogues while watching movies, interrupted with sudden bursts of baffling music. Soft berths on train chockfull of carpetbaggers, trading jeans, bras, live tortoises, and wild black rice. Xiang Wing is on business trip, tourist trip, investigative tour, purchase expedition, sales tour, family reunion, visit to exhibition, study tour, learning from others, writers' conference, sales exhibition, prize award ceremony, trip to summer resort, winter recession, cross-country networking, observation of others' work, taking part in competition, calling on old friends, nostalgic trip to historic sites, secret inspection tour, fleeing from arrest, a casual look around . . .

Stays in hotels guest houses elementary school classrooms community air-raid shelters basements public bathhouses train stations bus terminals under bridge arches in police lockups cages.

Then she arrives, finds, gets confused, goes stray, loses way, misses his destination.

Thereupon a fleet of motorcades in welcome ceremony present bouquets fires off popcorn salutes frantic waving of hands thunderous clapping. All swear he is a reformer a pioneering entrepreneur a shady dealer an upright man who petitions on behalf of the people a braggart a man who has strong backing from above, a man officially denounced. No one knows anyone else it can't find the person who is

160

supposed to meet the incoming guests and those coming to greet the arrivals cannot find the object of their mission. Applause scant and sparse, faces blank and without expression. Hence old comrades and the wives of old comrades hold his hands tight, "You haven't changed a bit," "You look much older," "I recognized you straight away," "I hardly know you." Then asks in a whisper whether he would like to buy some hawthorn plum ginseng. Then flings luggage on shoulder with a swing of the arm. And goes to counter to report loss of luggage.

He arrives to take up post and declares three principles of executive program at welcome meeting. She calls on the phone asking right and left for cheap lodging with good room good food good accommodations at minimal expense. Drawing a blank, it is at a loss for a good excuse therefore makes several urgent long-distance calls. She attends the first meeting of the reviewing committee and exhorts strenuously that award decisions not be affected by considerations of connections and juggling of claims. Soon after registration, when claiming meal stamps, he hands in his thesis written in both Chinese and English. It has all its organs checked, immediately receives injections of all newly developed newly imported drugs. He rushes from one government department to another demanding back pay and punishment of the libellers. It collects written audio video materials pores over them day and night listens to arguments and works on evaluations. She visits all old acquaintances former superiors paying homage to one after another by turns again and again. As soon as it arrives it began striving for a return ticket by bus ship horse dog running through all the tricks at fingertips, scampering madly three times in, seven times out.

Thinking this is indeed a lovely place, lake pleasing to the view, mountain crags soothing to the touch, inscriptions by celebrities, a feast for the eyes. Feeling the place lacks adequate management and proper maintenance, unbearably crowded, dusty, polluted, garbage everywhere. Changed beyond recognition, high rises, asphalt roads, on display in all department stores woolen sweaters made for export, styles and colors defies imagination and beyond human memory, makes one feel like being transformed into a gentleman or a lady from overseas. In the free markets are more duck tongues, swan combs, fish fins, and bear paws than are angels in heaven. Thinking it poor and shabby, wood replaced by cement without a piece of marble, so-called special private section, the cafe is only fit for taking cough mixture and toothache ointment. Young men with long hair unwashed for days and days look more like jailbreakers than hippies, ties dangling loosely and dirty collars exposed. No granite in any of the buildings not a single fountain not a single bronze statue. No sense of backwardness at all, not only calligraphy wave but symphony craze and Hexiangzhuang breathing exercises and arty gymnastics Chinese lion dance figure swimming falling on and off their feet and a young girl planning to set up an international stock company trading in bombers. Not only is there realism and revolutionary modern Beijing Opera but also modernism stream-of-imageism, Fie Fieism. Fei Fei Fei[1] is an acrobat entertainer at Tian Qiao,[2] Feng Fei Fei is a famous singer in Taiwan, and amid clamors of pipes and drums one or several black horses stud bulls piglets and male elephants are led onto the stage. Feels why not begin by building a few decent restrooms to prevent people spitting and pissing everywhere, always squeezing pushing bumping talking on the phone as if cursing, riding bus with expired monthly passes, drinking beer till throw up

1. In the original Chinese text, "Fie" and "Fei" are homonyms. The former means, "wrong" or "not," the later means "to fly."
2. Tian Qiao is a popular marketplace in Beijing, especially in olden times.

162

violently as seized by cholera, thirty cents deposit for a dirty plastic cup.

Then accepts invitations to opera, movie, song-and-dance, fashion show. To appreciate, understand, grasp, discuss, evaluate, judge, pronounce verdict, make ruling, help, cultivate, polish art. There are heated hubbubs and cool fade-outs, libido of the ancient Chinese sages and shriveling of human brain in the age of computers. There are sincere appeals cynical laughter and affected squeals. There are real explorations and fake airy inspirations, sincere running noses and phony eyebrows. Myriad critics, some entertained with savory lime eggs by artists, others spurned and spat on by artists, variously melancholy, calculating, slouching, shifty-eyed, or totally engrossed in work. And there is the newest challenge from the cliché-flaunting out-and-out bullshit awakened consciousness conscious of its own value.

Then word goes about that this art is innovative, is but worn-out puttee cast off by foreigners, is the sacrificial burial figure of the pre-Qin and Han dynasties, is a new blending of East and West aesthetic sensitivities like Costa Rica coffee with a dash of Napoleon brandy and aniseed used in Xingjiang kebab, is trapped in the old conventions of the forties and fifties, unable to break away, is incantation-like gibberish beyond even my comprehension, is the best Gold Monkey Gold Fish Gold Fan Award winner elected by popular vote, is a rock that blocks the path, a splendid burst of flora unprecedented in history, an open sewer that is breached too wide to be stopped up, is the new cross-eyed point of view, is a small topic under urgent discussion. Anyway he she it and they all applaud, then all dash away with loose bowels.

After discussions are receptions and banquets. Noodles in clear soup, eggs in chicken broth, garlic in ginseng soup, eels soaked in thick-skinned braggart's cowhide soup.

163

All propose toasts to Xiang Xing, Xiang Ying, in a word Xiang Ming with wine with vinegar with pepper mustard. Say so young yet so worldly-wise must be eulogized promoted worshiped a star of the new generation a breakthrough. The likes of them few and far between. Models for the twentieth or even the twenty-first century casting illumination faint or strong bringing cocaine bringing hormone bringing profundity bringing sense of the times bringing the future bringing Vogue of the Wild. Not to mention other benefits. Warning it's dangerous to go on like this lost directions halfway crash on mountain a thousand splinters a radiant big bang. Try as you may for breakthrough eventually ends in pissing in the Buddha palm[3] of Confucius being casted solidified smoothed out, achieve perfection of virtue, pass away peacefully, outmoded like what you get under a skullcap,[4] I mean, tails. Mumbling that in any case the moon in China is not quite round, except that he himself is more perfect than the holes in the sun. Muttering that it's better for you to concentrate on your own professional work not to make business trips or participate meetings, that you have to see more and hear more to be ingenious path-breaking passenger airliner of European Common Market. Declaring you're still not divorced your mind must be locked in a time capsule, that nowadays carnal desire overwhelming people no longer virtuous, that after all the heavenly laws should prevail and human desires suppressed, calligraphy of Kong Decheng,[5] Secretary of Council of Inspection in Taiwan, hang

3. An allusion to the classic Chinese novel *The Journey to the West*, in which the Monkey King jumps thousands of li away by a single somersault, and proudly urinates at the foot of a huge mountain, only to find that he is but moving on the palm of the Buddha.
4. Refers to the pigtail that men wore during the Qing Dynasty. Metaphor for that which is obsolete.
5. A direct descendent of Confucius.

high in Confucius' Mansion in his hometown Qufu. Even in Liulichang[6] in Beijing a Confucius Restaurant is open. Also sells roast duck. Will turn in grave if cut off in prime without having a meal there.

Xiang Ming can't help but raise the following questions! Is yolk good for you or does it give you heart disease? Can time passed be recalled? Which are more likely to rot— the new fashions or the old? Does proliferation of college diplomas mean progress in education, higher cultural level of the people, or the opposite? Are the words most frequently spoken the very things you most want to say and most enjoy saying? Smoking and taking expensive Chinese medicines and watching TV series, which would bring early death? Is bringing down others with abuses a proof of one's own superiority? Does it mean that one's speed is exactly right if some say one goes too fast and some say too slow? Is it a rule that a person who can speak English will find a foreign spouse and then help brothers-in-law to go abroad? Private enterprise, collective and state ownership, which has more initiative? How many of the talkers with high-sounding words are not charlatans? Traditional courtyard houses and skyscrapers, which is more modern? The linguist who invented the terms to distinguish special honored retirement from ordinary retirement, and "exoneration" from "rehabilitation", why does he not get an award? If the ancient and the modern people of today engage in a tug-of-war, who will win? The Centipede Gold Dragon kite and the Boeing 747 jumbo, which is the more awesome? He who does the talking and he who does the work, which is smarter? When is it easier to get upper respiratory tract infection, in winter or in summer? Which are more credible, funeral orations or daily speeches

6. A street in Beijing, well-known for dealing in cultural relics, antiques, books, calligraphy, paintings, etc.

at meetings? Downsizing the administrative body and expanding the staff, which is more effective? Martial arts fiction[7] and Scar Literature,[8] which is more sublime and heroic? Theorist and artist, which is the complete nervous wreck? Business trip or private travel, which is more costly? Will one return to the point of departure if one takes a hundred steps forward and then a hundred backward? Is someone with enteritis guilty of wasting food? Does checking into and out of the hospital have anything to do with health? Do non-poets non-painters and non-pianists necessarily know less about the poetry painting and music that poets painters and pianists do not understand? Which is the expression of love—I love you or I hate you? Foreign`Exchange Certificates or Renminbi,[9] which represents national cultural tradition? Which is more enterprising, to stay in isolation or to be in the heart of things? Water or wine, which is thicker? Art or money, which is more beautiful? Xiang Ming or Xiang Wing, which is more myself? Is the park a better place for breathing exercises, or a prison? The fake old diehard and the imitation foreign devil, which is the down-to-earth local product of Chinese culture? Is the new low-proof Yanghe liquor watered down? Does being awake mean not having any dreams? Do you assume that all foreign guests will invite you abroad? Does a person running hard mean there is a mad dog chasing him from behind? Is it adaptation or playwrighting to turn a novel into a film script? Who makes more, the worker or the idler? Are women necessarily beautiful and scientists naturally scientific? Are chopsticks wrapped in paper cleaner than those set on the table? Why mustn't one slurp when

7. Novels about martial arts masters, a popular Chinese literary sub–genre.
8. Late '70s and '80s popular fiction, exposing the Cult Revolution's victimization of ordinary people and their sufferings.
9. Foreign Exchange Certificate, supposed to be used exclusively by foreigners in China instead of Renminbi, the local currency.

drinking soup? Why should the Chinese follow Western table manners? How can one enjoy one's food without smacking one's lips? Is the flushing toilet more civilized than the chamber pot?

Stammering pouring out torrent of questions, he she it is expelled by electric prodder shown out politely led respectfully up the rostrum operation room seat of honor mortuary makeup room backstage. Granted Schill-Bel-Gondourt Award of International Geobiological Year 1982-328, listed in *Who's Who International* on the blacklist elected best male female boiled role . . . .

Xiang Ming thinks to himself, things nowadays are downright thrilling!

Capriccio à Xiang Ming
(A Sequel to "Thrilling")

That day Xiang Ming suddenly felt a little peculiar. Whether it was from a flight of fancy or a blight of flightiness, in any case he was feeling not a little thrilled. I am already a famous composer, he solemnly announced to his wife.

If Shiang Ming had announced he was a Persian cat his wife would have taken it in stride. Her equanimity gave one the impression she would have made an outstanding diplomat. More's the pity.

In that case I am going out to find a maiden from Huangshan. That is to say, a young housekeeper, a domestic service worker, a maid. Do you have any special instructions in this regard, Mr. Composer, sir?

Shang Ming thought for a moment, and then, with masterful insight, said:

You must get someone who is ugly, ungainly, unintelligent, unintelligible, and uneducated. You must remember this!

As he was going out the door, Shawn Ming added: And take away her I.D.!

He thought to himself that he was becoming pretty good at this.

Shaun Ming arrived at the Palace of the Imperial Consorts. The morning sun flitted over the surface of the water in the palace moat, shimmering like musical strings. The strains of Tchaikovsky's "Souvenir de Florence" floated into Sean Ming's mind. From his shirt pocket he took out a piece of sky-blue stationery, on which was a poem he had written for Cherie Sherry Sheri. He had spent more than five hundred centuries on the poem, but because he had neither the guts nor her address he had never managed to send it out. Folding the piece of paper into a boat, he cast it into the moat and jumped down after it, alighting on deck with the airy grace of a goose feather. From his perch in the vessel, he admired with a connoisseur's eye the sunlight glinting off the weather-beaten stones of the dilapidated parapets, and a feeling of great *mélancolie* filled his heart.

Jean Ming made one complete lap around the palace moat while he finished thinking out the structure and central motif of his next symphony. It would be known as the *Symphony in D Major*, "The Thrilling," Op. 92, and would have six movements instead of the conventional four: *Galloping Courante, Allegro Thrilling, Pedante (ma non troppo) Cantabile, Allemande Salamander, Recitativo Agitato*, and, finally, *Largo Molto Thrilling*. He kept this secret to himself. He had no intention of telling anyone, because his copyright and patent rights were at stake.

After that, he bought a ticket and went inside the Concubines' Palace. *Mama mia!* He had no idea it would be swarming with this many people, and worse yet, every last one of them a fellow *artiste*! It would have been less ominous had he run into an equal multitude of rats! No doubt this was his just dessert for having been so beastly about what he wanted in a maid. Hey hey! What what? Almost jumping out of his skin, he reeled around and began to run. Anything might happen in a crowd like this. Far better to be far from the madding crowd. Besides, artists should all be at home working away and minding their own business—what were they all doing milling around here? Up to no good, that's for sure. Next thing he knew he was being pursued, but the faster he ran the faster his friends followed, and the faster they followed the faster he ran. Finally, gasping and panting, he fell onto the ground and pretended to pass out, but then a heavenly host of Florence Nightingales descended upon him and began to administer a post-sauna-style heart massage. Laughing and crying, he got back on his feet and asked, in a quavering voice, What on earth is going on?

What his colleagues told him was this: When Ang-ang and Nao-nao announced some time ago that a case of the Bubonic Plague No. 1 had been discovered in the Concubines' Palace, the place became quite deserted for a while. Then Ang-ang and Nao-nao got together a ragtag bunch from somewhere and, calling themselves the Rat Patrol, armed themselves with axes and handsaws and DDT and 2-4-D and d-Con and melathion in sprays and fumigants and flamers and stompers and whatnot, and came to the palace and turned it upside down. On top of it all, they said that in order to do a really thorough job, they would have to remove the roof as well. From then on, nobody dared step foot inside the Palace of the Imperial Consorts, and Ang-ang and Nao-nao turned it into a giant casino. Not long after that, Ang-ang and Nao-nao got into a huge row over a car and actually came to blows with each other, this time turning the Concubines' Palace into a boxing arena. In the end, a team of experts from the Department of Health spent a year and a half taking samples and counter-samples for lab analysis, and then, with the United Nations World Health Organization providing assistance and authentication, finally concluded that there was no evidence of bubonic plague in the Concubines' Palace. With all this hullaballoo, how could those busybody artists—with their bloodhounds' noses for gossip and scandal—be expected to stay away?

As soon as Xiang Ming recovered from his fright, he

170

began to shake hands with each of his colleagues and fellow artists, whom he had not seen in ages, and inquired solicitously after everyone's health. They chatted affably for a while, exuding conviviality and camaraderie. But when he realized that the crowd was growing bigger and bigger, Xiang Bing thought to himself, of the thirty-six stratagems, the best one is to run away; speech is silver, silence is golden; to be ambitious and enterprising is good, but to let it be is superior. Whereupon he said, I have some matters I still need to take care of at the office, so please excuse me, I must take my leave now, take good care of yourself, hope to see you soon, good-bye, good-bye. And left.

No sooner had Xiang Bain stepped inside the main gates of the Cultural Workers' Association Building than he began to notice that all his colleagues and friends were whispering among themselves and exchanging meaningful glances, and he realized with a start that his plan to compose a "Thrilling Symphony" was already public knowledge. The scuttlebutt was that he was embarking on an extremely risky venture, one that would lead him straight into hell and high water. Astounded, Xiang Cain wondered, how did something I was just thinking about to myself become the talk of the town so quickly? Then one of his nameless bosom buddies told him furtively that an article severely critical of his "Thrilling" piece had appeared some time ago in some newspaper somewhere, wherein the writer pointed out that the composition exemplified the degeneration of Art and the corrupting influence of Western Modernism, that it had deviated from the correct path, and that it was guilty of this and that and so forth and so on.

Xiang Crain refused to believe it. So his friend, who shall remain nameless, brought him the newspaper in question, adding that it was out of concern for Xiang Crane's mental state and morale that he had not shown him the article when it was first published. Xiang Dane took the newspaper and gave it a quick glance. But what he found was a remarkable piece of criticism on something called "Thriller." Bursting into laughter, Xiang Duane said, my composition is entitled "Thrilling," the piece under criticism is called "Thriller." Anyway, what is this "Thriller"? Is it a suspense novel, or a children's adventure story? In either case, if it was indeed written in such a way that no one could make head or tail out of the tale, then it deserves to be roundly criticized, and even I will join in the denunciation! But what does that have to do with me? It's like confusing the Yuan Dynasty painter Wang Meng with the modern-day novelist Wang Meng—what on earth does one have to do with the other? Why then would anyone get the chills at the mere mention of the Yuan Dynasty Wang Meng? And, he asked, are there really such harebrained nitwits who would fire off their criticisms without first ascertaining what their target was?

He said all this with great bravado, but actually Xiang Meng's heart was pounding inside. His blood pressure shot up and down, his lips turned blue, then purple. He thought of Cherie.

Bosom Buddy No. 2 brought him another piece of news. Ang-ang was on a tear again, angrily and rabidly bow-wowing and denouncing Xiang Maine and creating a big to-do. But then, as a result of getting overly worked up, he soon fell into a swoon and collapsed onto the ground, foaming at the mouth and reeking of booze and rancid meat and other malodorous stuff, and had to be rushed to the emergency room at PD Hospital. When Xiang Lane heard this, he was overcome with sadness and pity. Everyone has feelings of envy at one time or another, he thought to himself, that's just human nature; but to be so overcome with envy as to endanger one's health and well-being, and, what's more, to incur such harm on account of a no-account fellow such as he,

Xiang Kane, was utterly ridiculous. After all, there was no reason why he and Ang-ang couldn't each seek his own particular brand of thrills and chills, and just stay out of the other's way. Besides, he wasn't even sure of his own name, some hotshot he was. The only difference between him and his soon-to-be-found housekeeper was in reality no more than just a matter of division of labor. To lose sleep over him, to become hospitalized over him, to become so passionate over him, wasn't that tantamount to carrying a torch for him, and carrying it too far? Even his own wife—he had never quite figured out how it was that he came to have a lawfully wedded wife—had never worked herself up over him, whether in passion or in anger. Could it be that Ang-ang loved him more than his own wife did? Wouldn't that be the ultimate in pervertedness!

At that very moment, a thunderous clangor of drums and gongs and a multitude of other instruments accompanied the arrival of one detachment after another of marchers who were parading right up to him, holding aloft a forest of banners with slogans such as: Warm congratulations on the successful completion of "The Thrilling Symphony"! Hearty salutations on the capturing of the Gold Medal at the Barcelona Music Olympics by "The Thrilling Symphony"! A solemn salute to the glorious composer of "The Thrilling Symphony"! . . .

While from the opposite direction another contingent of troops came bearing down on him, marching in goose step and with bayonets flashing, flanked by a formation of gray wolves on the left and of poodles on the right, and bolstered by armored personnel carriers amid a sea of banners that said: What is your real name? Resolutely help the thrilling writer change his class stand! No compromise is possible on cardinal issues of right and wrong! No cease-fire in the two-line struggle! . . .

173

Both forces seemed forged from invincible mettle, each one rushing forward like a tide that swept away everything in its path. Xiang King fully expected them to open fire at each other at any moment. Instead, to his complete astonishment, the two armies waved their banners at each other in a civilized, nay, cordial salute, and then joined together as one vast juggernaut heading straight for him, roaring:

We're going to get that chump Xiang Ling! Or:

Xiang Ning, this is the end of the road for you!

No no not I am not I am not I, I am not thrilling, I am not thrilled, I will never do this again, I am not in the least bit thrilling thrilled! Xiang Paine screeched as he wrapped his arms around his head and tried to scurry away. Cameras and flashbulbs whirred and popped. Reporters and paparazzi surrounded him six deep. The sharp whine of bullets arced above his head. Fighter planes and bombers dove in unison. Mercury guided missiles exploded one after another at close range all around him. Renminbi and even U.S. dollars rained down on every side, sloshing around until he could barely keep his footing. At that moment whom should he see right in front of him but Cherie Sherry Sheri? She seemed to have come from the Land of the Brobdingnagians. What a giantess she was! Xiang Twain began to scream: SOS!

She finally appeared, she, Cherie Sherry Sheri; she was a butterfly, a white bird. She was a fashion model. A public relations girl. She'd just come back from America with an advanced degree. She was working at a foreign venture funded by foreign capital. She was reclining on a neck- and back-massaging posturepedic pillow, a smile on her upturned face. What a beautiful come-hither pose! *Xing shi meili de!* (Sex is beautiful!) He couldn't help but be scared half to death, he would die without so much as a burial place. She leaped up like a flying fish, fished out a silencer and aimed it right at his heart, and poof!—

174

Xiang Wing somersaulted right into heaven, just like Sun Wukong, the mythical monkey king. Sun Wukong, . . . he murmured. He came to in an exotic new city. Rio de Janeiro? Casablanca? All the windows had been flung open for him, for his sake every last window was lit up. Tulips bloomed above the lighted musical fountains. In his honor every woman had tucked a shining white perfumed handkerchief into the top of her bosom. Boys were roller-skating down the boulevards. An old married couple kissed for an eternity beneath the ancient clock at the railway station. In the frigid air of an early winter's evening, the bronze statue of a composer who had roamed far from home silently endured the snow mixed with sleet. A crow began to sing the requiem, while from every direction came the shouts of money money money money money. . . . My dearest mother-like motherland! He wailed and wept until he passed out.

Xiang Ming finally woke up or perhaps fell fast asleep. He knew that all was well not well at all. He had no idea whether he was *Shorn Mane, Charlemagne, Germaine*, or *Shan't Name.* Was he a composer or a peddler of roasted sweet potatoes or a Communist comprador or a public security policeman or a restless ghost or a fabulous immortal or a clay figure that should have been put in a museum a long time ago. . . .

He laughed and cried and didn't laugh and didn't cry and and and and.

The Blinking of the Bell

My writing is constantly being interrupted by the ringing of the telephone. When the phone was first installed, I was ecstatic. I would never again have to stand outside a public phone booth, anxiously rubbing my hands and shuffling my feet, waiting to make some important call to some important place. A long-winded bullshitter or a coquettish young flirt would already have beaten me to the phone, and every sentence of their trivial gossip, nonsense, jokes, and endless digressions, not to mention their completely repetitious expressions and exclamations, would grate upon my nerves like a dentist's cleaning drill grinding upon a rotten tooth. And when I picked up the phone—often to make or return four or five calls at once—I would see that there would already be people lined up, waiting. I would feel that making a string of calls then would simply be inhumanely inconsiderate. Moreover, for every ten numbers you dialed, nine might not get through. Or even worse than not getting through, after dialing six digits, you might hear nothing at all, as if the telephone company had just been blasted out of existence.

I have given my wife endless grief and pain about making phone calls. So far in this half of my life, my success in troubling her outshines whatever I have done in writing or poetry. One time before she went to work, I gave her a piece of paper: she looked at it and started screaming. I also started screaming—you won't even help me with this little thing, you won't even show this little bit of loyalty, why, you can't even be compared with Song Jiang. You mean that I have to handle even these kinds of calls myself? Wouldn't that simply squeeze dry the last drop of my poetic inspiration? The numbers written on the card are 338888, 446666, 779999 . . . the numbers from 0 to 9 we humans have created are enough to punish us from one generation to the next. The writer's fee hasn't come in yet, the furniture order is nine months overdue, so why isn't there any news, excuse me but I can't dine with this Frenchman, the athlete's foot ointment from Foshan, Guangdong, has already been purchased, its arrival time is Thursday, 11:59 P.M.

When the phone was installed, I first dialed 117. 4:52. 4:52. 4:52:30 . . . 4:54. Then 123 . . . wind velocity increasing from level 2-3 to level 4-5. The wind is out of the EWSN. Then 113, long distance? No thanks. I almost dialed 119, we're on fire! 110, robbers!

Poet Zhao? Teacher Zhao? Little Zhao? Old Zhao? Comrade Ku-Yin? Guess who this is? You mean you can't even tell my voice? You son of a gun, have you become a damn section chief or something so that you won't even admit that you know me anymore? Hello, hello, hello, who's this? Aren't you the spun-wire factory? No. *You're* the spun-sugar yam store! Are you the Tian Yuan soy-sauce brewery? Is this the Donglai Shun Restaurant? Is this the west zone 4 Matchmaking Agency? Great Wall Hotel? The air-conditioning company? Cultural artifacts store? Hello, hello . . . even before getting up in the morning, or after having gone to bed at night, or just dozing off at noon, there's the ringing of the phone. You can't get any peace. Your poetic inspiration is gone. The attitude of someone who's dialed a wrong number is even more unreasonable than one who's dialed the right one—he simply won't believe that the phone is installed in your house or accept that your saying "wrong number." He won't believe that you are not the Accountant Zhang or Buyer Lee or Section Chief Wang whom he is trying to reach, but are simply you, your poem-writing self.

For the sake of my poetry, I smothered the phone with a cotton quilt. I protected the chrysanthemum-like purity of my poetry. The covered-up phone was so ugly—it was like covering the corpse of an illegitimate baby. The telephone possesses an especially ear-piercing kind of shrillness. It pierces through your inborn unfriendliness. It overcomes all kinds of obstacles to transmit to you some unfathomable bit of news. It doesn't give in to your inborn propensity for self-torment. It is guiltless and flawless, it doesn't have to get on its knees before your poetry or your cotton quilt. It assaults your conscience and sense of justice. It excites your curiosity. Maybe it's very important? Very urgent? Very unusual? Very interesting? Very useful? The sound of its ring seems to have changed again. Could it be a long-distance or perhaps even an international call from—the South Pole? Didn't I just finish a poem dedicated to the explorers of the South Pole? I suddenly thought that what lay under the quilt was a homemade land mine, its fuse hissing like a poisonous snake . . . ssz, ssz, ssz.

Many days have passed. I have learned how to answer the phone, to answer wrong numbers and the silliest calls. I have learned to harden myself and refuse its beckoning ring, refusing to take calls that I really wanted to get and thereby suffering the complaints of friends and relatives and the torments of my own regrets. I have learned to answer when I want to and refuse when I don't want to, or, refuse to answer when I really want to and answer when I don't really want to. Finally I picked up every call. This is because I write poems as soft as goose down. A poet's heart is soft and gentle. A gentle heart cannot possibly harden itself forever. Just pretend I'm not in. Just count me as not having been in at all. Let's just say that I am now at—the West Paracel Islands or the beer house downstairs. Would the ringing of the phone then still bring me pain and remorse?

But I am obviously still here. Yet I am conscious of my own existence, and by following the phone bell and phone line I become conscious of the existence of another person and his desire for conversation. Those desires should be sacred. What the receiver sends out is human language, not a neutron bomb. It's both moving and distressing. Just as there is no way I can refuse your hand when it is extended out to me, there is no way I can refuse a phone call. I give up. . . . I've finally learned to live alongside the phone. To live with its harassments and enticements, to live with the hopes and anger and the feelings of not knowing whether to cry or laugh that it brings. And also to write poems. Poems about the South Pole, the West Paracel Islands, beer houses, love, and even—the time spent alongside the phone.

Many days have passed again, and I have written quite a number of supposedly successful poems which for the most part are actually pretty awful. My phone has been replaced. On top there is a small device, and when a small lever is pushed down the phone no longer rings and all that remains is a light signaling.

So far I have not used this kind of modern equipment. I would rather respect and listen attentively to Mr. Telephone's news. This modernization is much crueler than muffling the phone with a cotton blanket. I am already over fifty years old and there is no way I can mold myself into a cruel person. Better to wait until after I am gone and then put into effect a modern anti-telephone or no-telephone campaign. A foreigner (from a modernized country) told me that his phone is equipped with a multipurpose computer. When he is working, the computer answers his calls. When the computer takes a call, it plays a recorded message saying, "The Mr. X you are looking for is not at home, please leave your name and telephone number, Mr. X will then return your call." The calling party then identifies himself and the computer automatically records the message. Amazing computer! It allows Mr. X to seize the initiative, to talk only with those he selects and decides are suitable to communicate with. When he gets tired of reading or sick of writing or exhausted from talking, or when his head becomes numb from thinking about his problems, then gentleman X turns on his answering machine and selects and returns those calls he ought to return, those he would find interesting to return, and chooses not to return those he doesn't need to or want to return or those he would find uninteresting to return. Isn't this also a matter of human rights? Who then could have known that the other party also uses a computer to control his or her calls, so when Mr. X returns a call to his beloved (for example) Miss Y, he also hears a recording: please leave your phone number . . . then there's no more person-to-person heart-stirring dialogue . . . only the calm, repetitious "conversation" of one computer to another.

This day has finally arrived. I have lived over fifty years, eaten so much food, taken so much medicine, worn through so many pairs of socks, all for this day. I've become a real poet. I, like my poems, am brimful and overflowing. I'm ready to risk everything, for you. I write new poems, I write about current events, I write about miners and astronauts, the Yellow Emperor defeating Chi-You, a successful self-taught person attains the rank of Number One Scholar, the cooperative enterprise Tai-Chi-Chuan, the White Swan Palace defeating the Cuban women's volleyball team, a specialized fishing household feeling estranged after obtaining a royal degree. I write about a Boeing 767 being promoted to the vice-ministerial leadership, the Eight-Diagram Company taking care of visas for privately funded students going abroad, people changing over to beauty pills because of textile import restrictions, Mohammed Lee's clear brother sheep head's phantasmagorical realism, Jia-ling-label motorcars discovering a new element, tomato-meat soup boiling, novellas being exempted from foreign-currency vouchers. I've forgotten everything, I praise history, reality, life, the domestic and the international. I praise this rambunctious energy of ours. I write while the telephone's electric bell loudly rings. I believe that every dong-dong du-du sound of the phone is trying to excite me, is beckoning me, so I turn off the little switch on the phone and write. I write that the Changlin diamond has been illegally lifted by a third party. I write about the weirdness of the weather, the boisterousness of life, the supply of goods cascading down like flowers from heaven. I've forgotten about the existence of the phone. I write about Peking ducks soloing in a hanging oven, dreaming of romance; Da San Yuan's roast piglets singing, "My ice-cold little hands" in Helsinki; the hopeless first love between socialist realism and stream of consciousness, having failed to get a housing permit, sadly parting. Dr. Omnipotent, expounding on the thesis that man must drink water, sweeping away all obstacles, defeating his debating opponents, then serving consecutively as the Olympic and National Championship referee; a quick-turnaround reselling nylon pantyhose free enterpriser getting to drink Yau Wen Yuan's dumpling soup; the disarmament agreement stipulating that outmoded hydrogen bombs be given to single sons and daughters; that steamed buns can cause cancer, and bread can teach Spanish typing through correspondence courses; the lover of Huo Dong Ge, commander in chief of the Opium War; Su-San dancing disco while en route to trial under guard and then later taking up fashion modeling; the Japa-

181

nese serial soap opera star being fined a month's bonus money after the dam broke. I beckon life!

Life beckons me. The telephone no longer rings; instead the signal bulb's green light blinks on and off, on and off, over and over again. It is wordless. It winks. How painfully it waits. Yet no, I can't, I and my poetic muse are already dancing in the air. It keeps on blinking, blinking for five minutes and then another five minutes. Its sound has been cut off by me, it is powerless, like a mute waiting silently for my attention. Perhaps the call comes from an old man who has been silent for a long time, and who, because of his keen insight, was able to discover something in my awkward poems that attracts him enough to want to talk to me. Perhaps it is transmitting some kind of invitation, inviting me to go to some verdant meadow? I don't dare go. Perhaps it's a protest, but then its mediocrity, its insignificance, its timidity, makes it seem that appearance and reality have separated. Perhaps it's merely the lonely call of a soul, the sound of some unrequited beckoning. You're crying? Perhaps it's a prediction, a curse, a report on someone's heartfelt feelings, the secret password "open sesame," or the shock of realization brought about in some baptismal ceremony. Perhaps it comes from outer space or perhaps from hell, from some banished deity[1] or a "San Lu" official from the Kingdom of Chu. On the other hand, it is still more likely that it is just a desert, a snow-capped mountain peak, a frozen river, or a desolate, lonely, remote concern from far away. It's the permanence that my poems and my life have lacked for far too long. It has a lot it wants to tell me. It wants to tell me about real poetry. And also about friendship. I have heard sounds from the blinking light of the signal bulb. I'm only afraid that after I pick up the telephone I won't understand what it's

1. The poet Li Po.

saying. But it's already too late, there's already no remedy, next life's poems are next life's problems. But I am good at smiling, equal to the task at hand, joy and anger do not easily show on my face. It is still blinking, it is still waiting, I didn't know that its patience was like steel, its enthusiasm like fire. It brings me deep, deep pain. I know if I answer this call my apartment will just collapse, the gas stove will leak smoke and the nanny will quit and all my poems will be consigned to flames. I will continue to write about life's burning passions, not only do I have thirty-six furniture legs made of kindling[2] and short circuits in my household appliances, but I also have you! I don't know how many pens I actually use when I write. I don't know what I have written. I don't know if my older brother will be able to forgive me this time. But I clearly see the green signal light insistently twinkling. Its deep concern for me, its sincere advice, its tenderness and expectations for me are all so refined and eloquent, yet mixed with a feeling of sorrow. That's the gleam of tears. Don't blame me! We share the same grief. Poetry torments life, the telephone torments poetry. Thus my tears fall like rain and I believe that poems will always have readers, that the muse of poetry will always be here, and the spirit of poetry will always be ardent, even if the bookstores aren't willing to order them.

2. A reference to the amount of wedding presents a couple might receive. For example, a bed might be equal to four legs.

Notes on the Author and Translators

WANG MENG was born in Beijing in 1934. Labeled a "rightist" in 1957 for a short story mildly critical of bureaucracy, he left Beijing to spend sixteen years in rural Xinjiang. His "rightist" label was removed in 1979, and he became a professional writer. Wang Meng was appointed Minister of Culture in 1986 and resigned after the Tiananmen Square uprising on June 4th, 1989. In 1991, his short story "The Stubborn Porridge" (1989) was attacked in the official journal of the Chinese Writers' Union, and Wang Meng sued the head of the journal for libel. In the fall of 1993, Wang Meng was in the United States on a coordinate-research program at the invitation of Harvard-Yenching Institute. This is the first collection of his short stories published in the United States.

ZHU HONG, Research Professor at the Institute of Foreign Literature, Chinese Academy of Social Sciences, in Beijing, she is currently a visiting professor at Boston University where she teaches a course on Chinese women's writing. She has translated and published two previous volumes of contemporary Chinese short stories.

YU FANQIN is a translator and editor at *Chinese Literature Magazine* in Beijing.

CATHY SILBER is a Ph.D. candidate in Chinese Literature at the University of Michigan.

AI-LI S. CHIN, a retired sociologist, is working on an oral history of Asian-American women in New England.

PERRY LINK is Professor of Chinese Language and Literature at Princeton University.

LONG XU is an Assistant Professor of Chinese at Furman University in South Carolina.

JEANNE TAI is a writer and translator in Cambridge, Massachusetts.

BENJAMIN LEE is Director of the Center for Transcultural Studies in Chicago.